One fo...
Three for a girl, four for a boy,
Five for silver, six for gold,
Seven for a secret never to be told . . .

for Silver

Jenny Oldfield

Hodder
Children's
Books

a division of Hodder Headline plc

First published in Great Britain in 2000
by Hodder Children's Books

10 9 8 7 6 5 4 3 2 1

Visit Jenny Oldfield's website at
www.testware.co.uk/jenny.oldfield

A Catalogue record for this book is available from
the British Library

ISBN 0 340 74408 1

Typeset by Avon Dataset Ltd, Bidford-on-Avon, Warks

Printed and bound in Great Britain by
Clays Ltd, St Ives plc

Hodder Children's Books
a division of Hodder Headline
338 Euston Road
London NW1 3BH

1

If you want to know my priorities, friends come pretty high on the list.

I mean, there's family – *numero uno*. My dad for sure. My mom maybe.

Then there's friends.

Not huggy, squealy, feely Rachel-Monica type 'friends'. Though, hey, I wouldn't say no to hanging out with Chandler. He's neat. I mean the guy has a sense of his own weaknesses (pretty rare in my experience) and terrible timing. And he has one of those 'Jeez, did I just say that?' kind of faces . . .

So how come I'm discussing prime-time TV when I should be focusing on my *real* friend, Kurt Silvermann?

Silver. That's what everybody in school calls him, except me and Carter.

Kurt's a silver spoon kid. Loaded. His family invented the expression, 'You can have it all'. Meaning money and looks. In giant helpings.

Duplex apartment overlooking Fortune Park in an art deco block almost as famous as the New York Chrysler

Building. Holiday homes in Colorado and Florida.

And the Silvermanns all look like movie stars. Perma-tan parents, Don and Karen, posing for the society pages strapless, backless, seamless, and wrinkle-free. A sister, Elouise, who married a Republican senator's son. And Kurt.

I'm not overplaying the guy's advantages; I really am not. And it's important that you should understand this and keep it in mind for what follows.

Friends. I call Kurt my friend, but not on the level of Connie, Zoey and Zig. And definitely not in the Joey Carter league.

OK, so define 'friend'.

A friend is a person you remember more than two facts about.

Someone who you know won't stab you in the back.

You can kid around with a friend.

They like the same movies as you.

You feel you might still want to be around them in five, maybe even ten years' time.

But the quality of friendship can vary from one individual to another.

Like with Ziggy, I'm comfortable. I see him putting his big foot in his mouth and he makes me smile. He's sweet with Zoey, buys her CDs and jewellery when it's not even her birthday. And Zig's not loaded, believe me.

Whereas with Connie, I have this love-hate thing. She stacks her CDs in alphabetical order and this drives me crazy. She wears studs in her nose and left eyebrow, which I see as her making a stand against the school authorities and admire. She's a weird mix; Goth girl meets librarian. Ever-changing hair colour to match her mood swings. So, not comfortable. But I want to be in the same room with Connie because life isn't boring when she's around.

Carter? Too complicated to talk about. Especially the attraction thing on top of the friendship. It takes away my ability to judge. I spend my time hiding the fact that I'm attracted to him because I'm scared it's stronger on my side than on his. Weird; I could free-fall out of a plane sooner than tell Joey how I feel.

Which is enough about friends. You can probably tell I'm avoiding the subject of Kurt Silvermann.

Kurt drop-dead-gorgeous Silvermann. Blue eyes, fair hair, the clearest, smoothest skin you ever saw.

Kurt will-he-won't-he-get-it-together-with-Connie Silvermann. She's like me and Carter; she won't say yes to a date with Silver because it looks too much like a commitment.

Kurt non-conformist Silvermann, addicted to the adrenalin rush of extreme sports. Show him an underground cave and he'll go down it, a rock face and he'll climb it.

Give him a rule and he'll break it.

Which is why, two days ago, I was walking down the corridor with him after he came out of the principal's office, listening to Kurt's version of the latest high crime and misdemeanour which he'd committed in the eyes of our beloved principal Mr Fiorello.

'Excluded!' Kurt laughed a genuine laugh, not the fake bravado kind. 'The guy actually excluded me from school!'

'Did you think you were immune?' I queried. I have this joke going with him that his family background gets him unfair privileges. I was kind of amused to find that when he was really up against it, it didn't.

'No. But, c'mon, I'm talking about Fiorello, remember!' Kurt swung round a corner towards the locker room. 'This is the guy who invented the Fortune City High School Success Lab. Nothing less than Grade A will do. "This is the school where students want to be!" For him to exclude me for skipping lessons kind of takes away from that, don't you think?'

'Is that what you did?'

Kurt grinned and nodded.

'How many lessons did you skip?'

'Not that many.'

'How many?' I made out like I was the stern parent.

'A whole semester of Theatre Studies,' he admitted.

4

'Every Thursday afternoon for eight weeks.'

'A whole semester . . . ?' I let my jaw drop and followed him to his locker. 'Weren't you just a little concerned that Miss Starr might notice?'

A shrug to show he couldn't care. 'Listen, Starr is a pain in the ass, and everyone knows it. Besides, I had better things to do.'

'Such as?'

'You know that new artificial rock face they built out on the university campus? I had to keep my regular appointment with a climbing instructor named Jeff Cotton.'

'You went climbing?'

'So?' To Kurt it seemed perfectly reasonable. 'Come the New Year, I plan to climb Pike's Peak with my old man. It's over 14,000 feet. I need to keep in shape.'

'So what was wrong with a letter asking for permission? Fiorello would probably have said yes. He might even have turned it into a press release: "Fortune City Student to Climb Fourteener!" ' I could see the guy doing it for PR purposes and the greater glory of his precious school.

By this time Kurt had collected his bag and was heading for the main exit. 'Not if it involved cutting Starr's lessons,' he bitched.

What was I missing? Kurt knew something I didn't, but I let it slide. I stood at the door, throwing the big question after him. 'So what will your parents say?'

(My dad would say very little if I got excluded, and his silence would be the thing that crucified me. My mom would scream down the phone.)

'Nothing I can't handle,' he threw back at me, angry that I'd asked. Like this was too real and raw.

And that was the last I saw or heard of Kurt: his lazy, loping walk down the drive towards his red convertible, him regaining his cool and giving me a wave as he drove off.

Until today.

Which brings me back to the subject of friends and just how much or how little you really know them.

Yesterday, Thursday, I stayed late to help with the school production of *Death of a Salesman*. This play, in case you don't know it, partly has to do with sons who lie to their father. Biff and Happy Loman. Willy thinks he brought them up right, yet they turn into liars and cheats who don't even know they're doing it. It's a classic. Also about the death of the American dream.

Connie takes the part of the mother. She worries about cheese and payments on the refrigerator, stuff like that. To see Connie tie back her hair and play the mousewife makes me smile.

'OK, Connie, this is the scene where you've finally had enough.' Miss Starr, dressed off-duty in a cerise silk shirt and tight black pants, climbed on to the stage for an intense piece of directorial intervention. 'The worm turns.'

Everyone paid attention, including Joey and me, who are only working the lights and sound for the production.

Starr fixed Connie with a close-up, energetic gaze, giving the impression she was six inches taller than Con, though actually she's shorter. 'You've been watching Willy go crazy over his god-awful job driving round the state trying to sell stuff that nobody wants to buy. You kept silent all the years your two sons bummed around, wasting every chance you gave them. But now they dumped him in that crummy restaurant and that's the last straw. You tell them to pack their bags and move out. OK?'

'Yeah. About time. Do I get to kick ass?'

'No, but you smack the flowers Biff brings you to the ground. And you shout get out and don't come back. OK?'

Connie grinned. It was the moment she'd been building up to all rehearsal. 'Great.'

So Starr backed off and told them to go ahead.

Carter and I watched the way Connie relished yelling words like 'louse', 'bum', 'animal' at the poor kid playing Biff.

'She sure scares *me*, 'Joey muttered, swearing to keep

out of Connie's way in future. He dimmed the lights on cue and brought a spotlight up on Austin Wainwright, who was playing Willy.

'Hey, it's only acting, OK?' I introduced the Ben music, low volume, steadily getting louder. Forget the Ben reference; it's not important. Oh, OK then. Ben is Willy's brother. You get his theme music whenever Willy is tipping over the edge.

By this time there was a small distraction in the empty theatre in the shape of the school principal, John Fiorello, who had come looking for Miss Starr.

Notice the word 'small'. My dad says it could be a key to Fiorello's personality. 'There's only one way to go for a guy who's vertically challenged,' he tells me with a grin. (My dad, Sean Brennan, is tall, laid back and looks like he walked straight out of some hospital drama. He'd be good in surgical-scrubs, saving someone's life.) 'And that is to prove that size doesn't matter!'

Specifically, Fiorello is under five-four, in good shape from working out regularly and eating a low-cholesterol, high-fibre diet. Strictly non-GM soya, if his wife, Mary Beth, has her way. He dresses well, smiles easily, has a firm handshake. What else can I tell you? He obviously sailed through the personality test they conduct at job interviews, coming out as well-organised, energetic, a born leader *blah-blah*.

Which shows you the value of the lousy test. Since

every student and quite a number of the staff at Fortune City High have John Fiorello down as a power-hungry back-stabber who twists everything around to show himself as the best school principal in the entire universe. He was the one who pulled the school around single-handed, he produces the best test results in the state, he leads a dynamic team of talented, hand-picked teachers . . .

Whereas, the truth is, if you knock on his door, he doesn't even know your name.

Oh, and he has practically no hair. What remains is dark and cut real short. Follically as well as vertically challenged. A lethal combination, according to my dad.

'Excuse me, Dyanne!' Fiorello interrupted Connie's big moment to call the drama teacher down into the auditorium. 'I need to confirm with you a couple of facts about Kurt Silvermann before I write officially to his parents.'

Kurt's name made us all pay attention. It seemed he hadn't been kidding when he told me that Fiorello threw him out. No one had seen him in school all day. Joey had tried to call him, but Kurt had switched his cellular phone to please-leave-a-message mode.

'. . . Absent from theatre studies for eight weeks?' Fiorello ran through the details. 'No assignments completed? Dropped out of the Arthur Miller production?'

Starr nodded three times. Obviously she was the one who'd gone to the principal about it in the first place. 'I cast him to play Biff; he looks right for the part and the kid has talent. But he only attended two rehearsals. After that he just never showed up; no reason, nothing!'

One small suspicion here; many of us felt that Starr had targeted Kurt more because he'd resisted her charisma than because she'd lost a great acting talent when he pulled out of the production. This teacher has a giant ego and doesn't like to have it dented.

('Me – one-time Broadway actress with larger-than-life past. You – boring little acolytes around a bright star.')

You either love Starr or loathe her. Connie rates her as a great drama teacher. I say she shows favouritism and treats some students unfairly. We argue over this.

In any case, Fiorello took Starr back to his office to help him compose his letter to Mr and Mrs Silvermann. Starr left us with instructions to carry on in her absence. Five minutes later, we were interrupted again by Mary Beth Fiorello looking for her husband.

Now Mary Beth is the mousewife housewife for real. Small, neat and dutiful. Two kids, Krystal aged eight, Nathan aged six. And a born-again Christian. Maybe ten years younger than her husband, she has good features but hides them behind the kind of clothes you don't generally see on women under sixty. Loose-fitting tunics, high collars, flat shoes. 'How come she dresses like that?' is the only interesting question you might ever think to ask about Mrs Fiorello.

'Mr Fiorello is in his office with Miss Starr,' Austin told her.

('Did you have to drag in Starr's name?' someone else asked after she'd gone.

The others laughed. Was I really and truly missing something? I promised myself to ask Connie about it.)

'No, he's not actually,' Mrs Fiorello said to Austin. 'I just came from there. There's no one in the office.'

'Sorry,' we mumbled. 'If he's not there, we don't know where he is.'

At the time, we didn't think much about it.

Connie picked up where she left off, 'kicking ass' as she put it. Carter concentrated on lighting the stage. Cue Ben music to show that Willy Loman had tipped over the edge into insanity and was about to die.

That was yesterday, like I said.

'Did you speak with Kurt yet?' I asked Carter earlier this morning. I was wondering how his parents had taken the news that he'd been thrown out of school.

Carter did his usual throwaway shrug. 'Nope.'

'Did you try?'

'Sure I tried. I went round to his place last night after we finished rehearsal.'

For a second I thought, *Well, why didn't you mention it to me? I would've come along*. But I held back. With Carter, stuff like that could be open to misinterpretation. Like, it could look pushy, not cool; whatever.

'With Connie,' Joey added, giving me a sideways look. It was lunchtime. We were in the cafeteria. Loads of noise, blobs of ketchup on the table, overflowing trash cans – disgusting. 'It was her idea to call.'

Hey, I thought. Connie could have dropped this into the conversation I had with her before class this morning. I was feeling kind of left out of the equation. Joey plus Connie equals . . . what?

'It was weird.' Carter misread my silence, rushing to tell me what had happened because he thought I must be worried about Kurt. Well, I was. But that wasn't what was going through my head. 'We went up in the elevator and rang the bell to the apartment. No response. Zilch. We went back down. The doorman said no one was home. Connie gave him a hard time for not telling us that before we went up. But the point was, the security guy looked kind of uncomfortable. His story was that Don and Karen Silvermann were away skiing.'

'Where?' I asked. Kurt hadn't mentioned that

his parents had gone on a trip.

'At a lodge they own near Boulder in Colorado,' Joey explained. 'The guy at the Roosevelt Building told us they left Kurt behind to continue his schooling – hah!'

'So where was Kurt when you called?' I wasn't exactly getting the jitters; more like small hairs lifting at the back of my neck. My suspicions were aroused, as they say.

'According to our guy on the door, he hadn't seen Kurt since Wednesday morning.'

'Which means he didn't go home after Fiorello kicked him out,' I figured. 'Even though there was no Mr and Mrs Silvermann there to ball him out.' Weird, since the last thing he told me was that he could handle his folks.

'Which may also be the reason why Fiorello had to write to the parents rather than speak to them on the phone.' This too slotted into place. Joey finished his fries and tossed the tray on top of the overflowing trash can, which Arnie Mercury, the site superintendent, soon cleared away. 'So Kurt took a rain check on the rest of his life.'

'Huh?'

'He failed to keep his appointment with destiny.'

'Carter, for God's sake!' I followed him out of the cafeteria.

'What I'm saying is, it looks like he chickened out

13

of telling his folks the bad news. He made plans not to be there when they got home – which, for his dad, is tomorrow by the way.'

'But why?' OK, so it was bad, but not that bad. Most of us can stand a parent screaming abuse at us for an hour or two. Where-did-we-go-wrong? Why-did-you-shame-us? The sooner you get out of here and take responsibility for your own life the better! And so on.

Joey gave the annoying shrug and walked off.

So I grabbed Connie and twisted her arm for her theory on Kurt.

'OK, so it looks like Happy Families with the Silvermanns,' she told me. This was during social science with Mr Nelson, so we had to whisper. 'Squillions of dollars, big apartment, partying with the beautiful people . . .'

'. . . But?' (Wow, was there a lot I didn't know about people in general, I realised.)

'But Momma has an alcohol problem,' Connie hissed.

'No!'

She nodded. 'Kurt told me. It goes way back. Forget the skiing in Colorado story; Karen Silvermann is currently in rehab. And Elouise, the sister; her marriage is on the rocks.'

'No way!'

'Yeah. He told me in confidence, OK? If you must

know, that whole family is falling apart.'

'So you reckon Kurt decided not to stick around for the happy homecoming tomorrow? But if so, where did he run to?'

'Now *that* I don't know,' Connie answered hurriedly, before Mr Nelson came down heavy on us.

So where did Kurt decide to hole up after he drove out of school in his red convertible? That was the main mystery.

Until a bigger mystery took its place, to do with Fiorello. Which is the main thing I keep putting off telling you about.

2

The only reason I got involved with *Death of a Salesman* was Kate.

I'd like to clear that up from the start.

I mean, acting isn't my thing. Like, if you asked me, 'What's the worst job in the world?' I wouldn't answer 'Street cleansing,' or 'Used car salesperson'. It would be 'Actor', without a doubt.

You have to learn someone else's lines and stand up in front of people. On a platform, with lights. You get one word wrong, you have a nose a millimetre too long or poor orthodontic work on your front teeth, they rip you to shreds.

I can sit backstage and watch other crazy guys putting themselves through that kind of torture. But as for getting up there myself, forget it.

Starr was pushing Connie and Austin around the place, showing them how to get into a convincing clinch.

'Don't hold him like he was a shop-window mannequin!' she told her.

She was gonna demonstrate the technique herself, I could tell.

'Remember, Willy's your husband of more than thirty

16

years. He's a broken man. You have to be tender with him, like this!'

Can you picture being married to someone for thirty years? That's what I mean; this acting stuff calls for too much imagination. I watched Starr get into the clinch with Austin, who didn't look like he was having much fun either, to tell you the truth.

'Hey, man, you got a minute?'

This was Arnie Mercury calling me away from the lighting board.

('Hey, man, you ready for the shock of your life?' as it turned out. Only Arnie didn't know it at the time.

Leastways, I didn't think he did.

I blame Kate. If it hadn't been for the fact that she was doing the sound, I wouldn't have been there. The site superintendent would have had to ask someone else if they had a minute.)

I looked at Miss Starr enthusiastically rehearsing the kiss with Austin Wainwright. 'Yeah,' I mumbled, glad to be out of there.

'Do you need me too?' Kate offered. No sound effects required while characters embrace.

'Sure, why not?' Arnie gestured for us to follow him.

He was a quiet guy, pretty new around here. Never had a lot to say. So I had to ask him what was the score.

'Principal's office,' he told me.

Which didn't help. Kate pulled some kind of face

17

behind Arnie's back. Like, 'Thanks a lot, Arnie, for that clear explanation of the favour we agreed to do for you!'

All we knew was we'd turned left down the corridor towards Fiorello's room.

'You got a problem?' I prompted.

'Looks that way.'

'You care to describe it to us?'

'Door's jammed shut.' Arnie was the type who never gave anything away, not even an unnecessary word. He's thin; his nose is sharp like a beak. You could think his black, glossy hair stands up from his scalp like the crest of a bird.

There was no point carrying on with the conversation to ask what was jamming the door, or why Arnie needed to gain entrance. Easier just to wait and see.

Approaching the principal's office made me think about Kurt and what Kate had told me about his being excluded. And about the fact that he didn't go home after Fiorello delivered the fatal blow.

Sure, he's the kind of kid who can take good care of himself, don't get me wrong. And he always carries the dough and a cell-phone to get himself out of trouble. It's just that his absence threw up a few questions. And Connie was worried about him.

I was into wondering how worried Kate would be about me if I chose to go missing (probably she wouldn't lose much sleep, but she might go around to my place to make a point of asking my parents or my sister what they knew), when the principal's cream panelled door brought me into present time.

'Jammed,' Arnie showed us, turning the handle and pushing against the door to prove his point.

True. It was unlocked, but there was some object rammed up against it.

'How's the cleaning company gonna gain access tomorrow early?' Arnie wanted to know. It was his job to worry about stuff like that.

'Did you try looking in through the window from the outside to see what the problem is?' Kate suggested. Always logical.

Arnie nodded. 'The blind's down.'

'You want us to help shove the door open?' I worked out the probable reason why we were there.

'The cleaner's gotta get in.'

'OK, so we push.' There was enough movement to suggest that brute force would clear away the obstacle on the inside of the door. Picture a wooden chair propped up against it, or the shaft of a broom; something like that.

Birdman Arnie was skinny but muscular. I'm skinny, period. Kate's pretty sporty. None of us were the type to score high marks in the brute force department, so it was a question of applied technique.

Arnie put his shoulder to the edge of the door. I got ready to ram it with the sole of my boot. Kate likewise.

'Ready?' Arnie asked.

We nodded. He shoved, we kicked.

The door opened a half inch.

'Mr Fiorello?' Kate said, trying to peer through the gap. No answer, which was predictable. Even Arnie must've tried the approach of calling out the principal's name to see if he was in there. 'Why would he do this?' she wondered.

I shrugged. 'Again?' I asked the bossman, birdman, Arnie.

He nodded, like a sleek black hen pecking the dirt for scraps of grain. 'Ready?'

Shove, kick, kick.

We gained another fraction of an inch, but this time the object rammed against the inside of the door caused the panel to creak and splinter.

'It's gonna split!' Kate breathed, pushing her long dark hair back from her face and taking a deep breath.

'Yeah.' One problem solved. If we broke the door panel, one of us could stretch inside and remove the obstacle. At least we'd be in, with only minor damage.

So we booted it another couple of times.

Crack!

Did you ever hear wood splinter and tear? 'Crack' doesn't cover it, but you get the idea.

So, anyway, there's a jagged gap in the panel and the shaft of some garden implement or workshop tool poking through. It's a smooth, shaped, wooden handle.

And it's not dry. It's sticky and red-wet.

'Oh, God!' Kate gasped.

('Gasped' doesn't cover it either. It was a dry, shuddering intake of breath. Shock-horror.)

Arnie Mercury stepped back and leaned against the opposite wall of the corridor.

So it was down to me to continue.

But there was no way I was gonna take hold of the handle of that hammer, axe or whatever it was. Not because I knew it might destroy fingerprints or upset the forensic guys once they arrived on the scene. But because I was in shock too.

I mean, that red-wet stuff was obviously blood.

I didn't want to touch it, so I used my foot to do more kicking of the broken panel. Pretty soon it caved in and the blood-covered handle fell against my leg. I shot back like the thing was red hot.

Which put me in a position against the wall next to the more than usually silent site superintendent. From here, if I stooped down, I would be able to peer through the broken door.

'What is it?' Kate begged in that same dry, gasping voice. 'What can you see?'

I stooped.

A body. A face staring up at the ceiling with dead eyes. A grey suit and a white shirt stained red. More red on the carpet.

21

'Joey?' Kate pleaded.

'It's Fiorello,' I told them. 'Someone just hacked him to death with an axe.'

You don't mess around. You call the cops and the paramedics. They arrive to take control, and that's when it hits you.

The siren penetrates the shield of numb trauma that blood and a sharp steel blade induces. Well, it does in me, and I could see that Kate and Arnie Mercury were suffering from pretty much the same condition.

We hung around in the corridor without saying anything, without going back to the theatre to inform the others, with blank stares on our faces.

Nyaah-nyaah, nyaah-nyaah! Blue flashing lights kick your brain into action. Uniforms bring back the power of speech.

'Over here!' I yelled at the first cop through the main door.

He ran with his gun pointing straight at the principal's door, right arm rigid, left hand supporting the arm under the elbow.

'Out of the way, you kids!' More officers swarmed into the building, similarly armed.

It hit me then that the axe-wielder might still be in the room. Maybe he barricaded himself in there with the corpse. So I obeyed the order and pulled Kate down the corridor to let the cops deal with him.

They surrounded the door, which stood a few inches open, the shaft of the axe still poking through the broken panel. I counted five guns aimed at the doorway.

And by this time, the cop sirens had brought Miss Starr and the kids at the rehearsal running along the corridor.

One officer split off to intercept them. I saw him speak urgently to the teacher and kind of herd the group back. Miss Starr resisted, so he picked her up and dumped her in the secretary's office, with strict orders to Austin not to let her out.

Meanwhile, the first cop on the scene used his gun to poke at the door.

It eased open far enough for us to see more of the body, and the fact that the whole room was trashed. Lights were smashed, chairs overturned, a computer screen shattered, and blood had splashed up the pale blue walls, like some crazy artist had been at work.

Kate hid her face in her hands. Nightmare.

Arnie was blinking his beady bird eyes. Blink – this can't be happening – blink. He acted like he was trying to make himself invisible from the cops, pressing himself back against the wall.

The first cop followed his gun into the room. He pointed it into every corner, stepping over the murder weapon and carefully avoiding the corpse.

No axeman. The other cops piled in to confirm the fact

23

that Fiorello was the only person there.

To my mind, though, a corpse is no longer a person. It's a vacancy, a shell; and in this case one that was damaged almost beyond recognition. Except for the smart grey suit and the small stature of the guy on the carpet.

'Can you confirm ID?' the cop in charge asked us, as another officer radioed for forensic to attend the scene. 'Is it the school principal, Mr Fiorello?'

I was the one who said yes, not Kate or Arnie.

My brain was functioning OK, but I still wasn't feeling too much. I guess that's how cops do their job; they have a way of switching off their emotions and remaining objective. With me right then, it wasn't a conscious decision, more a defence mechanism.

I was telling myself, *Fiorello's dead. And it was messy. There was a fight. The guy with the axe won; well, he would. He most likely jammed the door closed with the murder weapon, then escaped through the window. Or else through the door that interconnects with the secretary's office, a fact which seemed to have escaped Arnie's attention.*

(I could hear Dyanne Starr screaming the place down as the news filtered through.

'Oh, Jesus, no! It can't be! John! . . . Let go of me! John!')

'You OK?' I checked with Kate, realising for the first time that this was an incident people might get upset

24

about. Like I said, I was a million miles away from feeling stuff myself.

She shook her head. 'Joey, this is awful!'

'Can we leave?' I asked the sergeant, for Kate's sake. She was shaking all over. Her voice was a whisper.

He didn't give the request much space. 'We need a statement from everyone involved.'

Involved? How come being in the wrong place at the wrong time meant we were involved?

Inside the room, the excitement seemed to be over. A corpse, but no suspect present at the scene. Four cops were returning their weapons to their holsters and congregating in a corner away from the main action.

'Can we sit down?' I asked. If we didn't find a chair, I was pretty sure Kate would soon be out of it; the way she was trembling, and the colour of her face. She's tough in her head, the way she thinks, but sometimes she overestimates how much her body can stand.

'Put them in with the others,' the sergeant instructed one of his men. 'And contact the next of kin. I take it the guy has a wife?' he asked me on my way down the corridor. I was supporting Kate with an arm around her waist.

('Oh, John, for God's sake, no!' Miss Starr was still groaning and whimpering from the secretary's office.)

'Yeah,' I told the sergeant. 'He has a wife and two kids. They live on Constitution Square, across the plaza from Kate.'

25

3

'This makes me into a horrible person,' I said to anyone who happened to be around.

It included my dad, Joey Carter and Connie, who came over to my place as soon as the cops took her statement and let her leave.

Trauma had addled my brain and done something to my nervous system that was making me shake all over, even three hours after the event. I was sitting cross-legged on the floor; Connie had her arm around my shoulder.

'How come you're horrible?' she murmured.

'Because I don't care about Fiorello!' I'd been asking myself how I felt about how our school principal met his end, and though the blood and stuff had really got through, the fact that the guy was dead hadn't touched me. I still thought of him as the grey suit, the cheesy, corporate figurehead, high on spin, low on substance. 'You see; I'm not nice!'

'Hey, forget it,' Connie told me. 'Fiorello didn't come across as Mr Nice Guy. You can hardly blame yourself for feeling this way now he's dead.'

'Yeah,' Dad agreed softly.

'What do you think?' I asked Carter.

He was sitting opposite me, staring right into my eyes, his knees almost touching mine. For a few seconds he didn't give me an answer.

'No, forget that. I mean, how do you feel?'

He shrugged. 'Like you; I'm not gonna lose sleep.'

This was as close as Joey got to talking about dangerous stuff like feelings. I was grateful for this much at least. 'But what about his wife and kids?'

'Yeah.' Carter sighed and stood up. 'I feel more sorry for them.'

End of conversation.

Which is why, after Carter and Connie had left and there was just me and Dad in the house watching late night TV, a ring on our doorbell and the arrival of Mr Fiorello's widow put me back several hours on the uncontrollable shaking front.

'Can I come in?' Mary Beth Fiorello asked my dad.

Too surprised to answer, he stood to one side and she stepped into the hallway.

I mean, the Fiorellos have lived across the square since he began the job at school, which is probably two years. We've seen them to say hi to, watched her piling the kids in and out of the car, but mostly I've avoided having conversations.

27

'I don't mean to disturb you.' Mary Beth stood there, apologising. Her husband had just been killed with an axe, for Christ's sake.

'No, you're not. Come in.' Dad made up for me by taking her by the elbow and leading her into the living-room. He was kind, but not too kind; not drowning her in sympathy but more waiting to take his tone from her. He sat her down, offered her a drink, which she refused.

'I just came from the mortuary,' she told us calmly. Was it calm, or was this her version of the traumatised daze? It was hard to tell. In any case, her pale, round face was impossible to read, like she was freezing all expression and imposing some distance on events. 'I had to ID the body.'

'Do you need me to call someone?' Dad asked. 'Your parents? A counsellor?'

She shook her head. 'My sister is in the house, taking care of Krystal and Nathan. I have all the help I need, thanks.'

'This must be terrible for you.' Dad felt his way. He looked like he was scared that Mrs Fiorello might suddenly cave in.

'Yes.' The same blankness. But not much danger of her tipping over into hysteria, I didn't think. The word I was thinking was 'control'. It was pretty spooky, actually.

Imagine. Your life just fell apart in the most violent

possible way. Someone hated your husband enough to hack him to death with an axe. I'm sorry to push the brutal truth in your face, but, as I said, picture it.

That person, whoever he was, robs you of your future. Your kids have no father. And you sit in a stranger's living-room, hands resting in your lap, palms upwards, you're breathing normally, you're composed, your hair is neatly combed, you even remembered to button your coat before you went down to the mortuary to identify his body.

It's weird. But that's what Mary Beth Fiorello was doing right then.

' "The Lord giveth and the Lord taketh away," ' she remarked quietly.

Oh yeah. I'd forgotten she was majorly religious.

If you're not, like me and my dad, there's not a lot you can say by way of reply. So we sat and waited.

Like, why was Mary Beth here?

'I'd be the first to admit that we're in God's hands,' she went on, 'and that He works in mysterious ways. When the Lord decides to gather you into His arms, then we must praise Him and thank Him for his goodness.'

Personally, I didn't see how much God had to do with an axe and blood sprayed over the walls.

But I was glad He offered Mary Beth comfort, big-time.

'Of course, it doesn't block the grief,' she went on, kind of contradictory. 'And Jesus wouldn't want it to. We grieve the departure of our loved ones, and still we glory in their ascendance to heaven to sit at God's right hand.'

Dad glanced my way to see how I was taking this. My hands were shaking hard, actually. 'What can we do?' he asked the widow, trying to stick to practicalities.

She looked hard at him without the shadow of a tear in her clear grey eyes. 'Mr Brennan, I want your daughter to help me identify my husband's killer.'

Forgiving your enemies wasn't high on Mrs Fiorello's agenda right then. No sir. She'd come to ask questions.

'Kate, you were there . . .'

'Yeah, but I don't know a whole lot.' Wrong place at the wrong time, that was all. *Don't involve me*.

You are involved. That cool grey stare seemed to penetrate my thoughts and counter them. It dragged me in. 'Just tell me; who raised the alarm?'

'That would be Arnie Mercury, I guess. He couldn't open the door to Mr Fiorello's office.' (Weird to be speaking the guy's name, having seen his corpse.) 'When he turned the key, ready to give access to the cleaning company, the door was jammed. So he came for help and found me and Carter.'

'Carter?'

30

'Joey Carter. He's doing lighting for the production.'

Mrs Fiorello made a mental note then nodded at me to continue.

'That's it. We got there and decided to force the door. Then we called the cops.' I was reliving it and it wasn't pleasant. I'd come up in a cold sweat.

'Why didn't Arnie think to get in through the interconnecting door from the secretary's office?' Cool as you like. 'According to the police sergeant, that door was open all along.'

'I guess it just didn't occur to him.' Arnie Mercury didn't strike me as big in the brains department. Maybe I was undervaluing him, I don't know.

'Also, according to the sergeant, the axe came from Arnie's store-room in the school basement.'

My dad and I stared at her. By now we were pretty much open-mouthed. 'Do they think Arnie did it?' Dad asked.

'Too early to say.' Mrs Fiorello studied the smooth palms of her hands. She was about 35, did I say? Her jacket was dark blue, good quality cashmere or some such soft, warm fabric. She wore a red and blue silk scarf, and that top button neatly fastened. 'It's possible in a practical sense that he committed the murder and then covered his tracks by pretending to come looking for help to open the door. That would give him witnesses – you and . . . Carter, was it? – to the discovery of the body, and he could act like it was the first he knew of it in front of you, to throw everyone off the scent.'

'That takes a whole lot of nerve,' Dad pointed out. 'And a high level of premeditation. In other words, is Arnie Mercury capable of killing in cold blood then covering up his tracks as coolly as that?'

A sigh escaped; the first sign that she was suffering. 'Not in my opinion. No, Mr Brennan; if the police follow that line of inquiry, I'd say they were wasting their time. For a start, they'd have to match the bloody footprints on the carpet with shoes belonging to Arnie.'

'Footprints?' I repeated. A touch of the OJ Simpsons here. The tread on the sole of the killer's shoe. Next Mrs Fiorello would be telling us they'd discovered a discarded leather glove and Arnie Mercury would be driving down a freeway with police choppers circling overhead.

'Yes. And forensics would be looking for DNA traces in his apartment. No one can clean up that good after they've committed a brutal murder.'

'You think it's all a little too obvious?'

She nodded. 'Not only that. I happen to know Arnie. He's a member of my church.'

Silence from us, during which we noted that if the guy was a true, born-again Christian, it would look kind of strange to keep him in the frame.

And Mary Beth seemed to have someone else in mind. She swung the conversation around. 'Kate, my next question is: how did the others react?'

The others? What others? There was Carter. As I remember it, he was mainly taking care of me. The kids from the rehearsal: Austin, Connie, the rest. They'd been cooped up in the secretary's room. Oh, and Dyanne Starr. 'Miss Starr was pretty upset,' I told Mrs Fiorello.

('Oh, John, for God's sake, no!')

She seized on this and wanted to know the details: how long before the theatre studies teacher showed up on the scene, her exact words and so on.

And then she let drop the fact that the police were already interested in a recorded message on Fiorello's machine. One particular voice belonged to a man identifying himself as Don Silvermann, Kurt Silvermann's father, calling from Boulder, Colorado. Mr Silvermann wanted to set up an appointment to meet Fiorello the following Monday, after he got back into Fortune City from his skiing trip.

'So?' I prompted. This meant that Kurt, wherever he'd been hanging out since Wednesday, had in fact been in touch with his father.

'So, the meeting was apparently concerning Kurt's exclusion from school,' Mrs Fiorello explained.

33

'Which the police sergeant I was talking with saw as maybe some kind of lead.'

No way! Were they crazy? Kurt? I stood up suddenly and paced the rug.

'He said, sadly it's not unknown for kids with grudges to go berserk on campus and take their revenge.' Mrs Fiorello got up too. 'Do you know the Silvermanns?' she asked.

I stared at her. What planet was she living on? Everyone in Fortune City knows the Silvermanns. They're like the Kennedys are to New York, neo-royalty, Princess Di, Prince Charles, or as close as we get.

Gently my dad filled her in. He said that Kurt hadn't been seen since Wednesday, so not to build up her hopes that he was a viable suspect.

She took this in, thanked us for spending time talking with her, said it had helped settle her mind about certain issues.

Dad showed her to the door, offered her an umbrella to cross the square in the cloudburst that had started since she arrived. 'If there's anything else we can do . . . really!'

The rain splattered down on to the umbrella. Mrs Fiorello looked out from under it, plain and scrubbed and beautiful as a madonna in a church painting. The hall light cast a yellow glow over her pale face with its frame of thick, wavy, dark brown hair.

'Thank you, Mr Brennan,' she told him.

I swear I heard a touch of triumph in her voice during what she said next. At any rate, a certainty that made unbeliever-me rock back on my heels.

'I put my trust in Jesus to see us through this terrible time. Jesus loves and protects us. With His help, I feel sure we're gonna make it.'

4

The day after Fiorello got killed, Kate and I were involved in a pretty heavy discussion.

OK, an argument. While we were picking our way along the busy sidewalk.

She said maybe it wasn't possible for one person to know another; not really know.

I said that was stupid. Some people were real close.

'Like who?' Kate challenged.

'Corny, but like my mom and dad. They're a complex form of symbiosis; they don't need to talk or be in the same room to know what the other is thinking.' Point proved. Even Kate would have to admit that.

'Leave out married couples. They share a lifetime's bad habits, no big deal. But take friends. Name me two who really, really communicate!'

'OK. Me and Zig.' Why was she pushing this line? Was it her way of telling me that a serious relationship between the two of us was never gonna happen? This suspicion upset me, especially given the fact that I'd gone into the lighting work for the school production solely because of Kate, and had felt pretty close to her only the night before.

She narrowed her eyes, walked ahead, then turned to wait. 'You and Zig only ever talk about sport, right?'

'Mostly, yeah.' I checked a little way further ahead to make sure Connie and Austin weren't catching any of this. I was feeling raw. I could do without any pressure from Kate.

'So basketball and baseball aren't exactly world-shattering topics of conversation.'

'Yeah, but it's not that simple. Talking basketball to Zig isn't just about tossing a ball into a net. There's other stuff going on under the surface.'

'Such as?'

'Y'know.' I shrugged. Bonding stuff. Guy stuff. I didn't feel like explaining.

'No, I don't know. Tell me.'

'Hey, what's with you this morning? What's all this about?' Great, Carter; a nifty little sidestep – not!

'Friends!' She raised her voice, making Connie glance back. Luckily, a delivery van dropping stuff off at the pizza place on the corner of Sixteenth Street drowned out what we were saying. But then a 'Don't Walk!' light flashed and made us bunch together at the kerb. 'I'm asking, how can we be sure that the way we think about someone else is correct? Maybe every judgment we make about each other is based on wrong ideas.'

'Hey, Kate, that's heavy!' Connie jumped in with both pointy-toed feet. 'It pretty much leaves us all stuck in our own little worlds, period.'

'Yeah.' Kate looked at the ground and almost walked out into the traffic.

The fact that I stuck out my hand to grab her arm and pull her back didn't strike her as ironic at that point.

'I mean, what do any of us know about Kurt, for example?' she went on. Clearly she'd been thinking about this non-stop for some time. 'We know what he wants us to know, that's all.'

'No; we also know what the newspapers and magazines tell us about his family.' This was Austin's contribution, demonstrating a touching faith in the printed word. I think Miss Starr chose him for the part of Willy Loman because he was born forty-five years old, mentally and physically.

'Back off, Austin,' Connie muttered. 'What got into Kate?' she mouthed at me. I shrugged back. 'I'll tell you what I know about Kurt,' she told Kate, figuring out faster than me what was bothering her, at the same time disproving Kate's every-man-is-an-island theory. 'I know he didn't kill Fiorello.'

'I never said he did!'

(Much too sharp and fast and defensive. Wow!)

'No, but it's what you're thinking,' Connie told her.

We were walking the last stretch towards the school gates, under the Circle Train route. Saturday morning, so no crowds of kids hanging around the gate. Just cop presence in the form of orange tapes across the main entrance and some scientific guys coming and going in white overalls. Forensics, I guess.

Kate: tall, dark hair tied back, slim, having a grey day, i.e. narrow, grey trousers, big grey sweater made of hairy wool; versus Connie the Goth: shorter, much more colourful, spikier, shinier.

'Are you telling me what I'm thinking?' Kate challenged, face to face.

'Kurt didn't do it!' Connie repeated.

'It's not me, it's Mrs Fiorello who thinks that!'

And that's when it all came out, just before we went into rehearsal on the Saturday morning; the message that Don Silvermann had left on the principal's machine, and the grudge interpretation the cops had put on that exclusion thing, which they had swiftly passed on to the widow, who had come to see Kate and her Dad . . . and so on.

No way!

Kate told me that had been her first thought. No way was Kurt the violent type. He was so laid back he almost fell over. He couldn't possibly work up that amount of rage.

'But I had a night of not sleeping on it,' she confessed. 'This morning I wasn't so sure that I knew even the first thing about the guy.'

'What are you saying? You think we've all got lousy judgment, not just you?' I tried to point out on a light-hearted note the fact that Kurt was a popular guy, despite his good looks and squillionaire dad. 'What do they say, "You can fool some of the people some of the time, but you can't fool all of the people all of the time"? Or, should that be, "You can fool some of the people all of the time, but . . ." '

'Joey, back off!' Kate pushed me away from her sound-board. She was over her argumentative stage, a smile was breaking through. OK, I realised; that hadn't been down to me after all. That had been the post-traumatic stress kicking in, and now she was over it, thank God. Kate and I were still good.

We came up to a cue for Ben music and Starr was giving us The Look. Willy was still raving about finding diamonds in the jungle, just before the sound effect for a car engine starting and moving away at full speed.

That's when Willy finally kills himself. Don't expect a bundle of laughs out of this year's school play.

So there were a lot of crashing chords and bashing drums, then a cello playing all by itself (multi-talented Miss Starr had written the music). Connie came offstage, wrung out like a rag after all that expenditure of emotion. And we're not even talking real-life here.

'It looks like you were wrong about one thing.' Kate still had her eye on the Silvermann ball.

'Give it a rest,' Connie pleaded. She slumped on to a chair beside my lighting console, tousling her Mrs Mouse hair style into its more normal shaggy mane.

'No, you remember you said forget the skiing trip, Mrs Silvermann was in rehab – all that?'

'Yeah, right. Kurt gave me the low-down.' Connie glanced at me. 'Close your ears, Joey. This isn't for you.'

You listen twice as hard when someone tells you that. It was the first I heard that Kurt's family had problems the same as everyone else.

'Well, it's not true. Mr Silvermann called Fiorello from Boulder, deep in the Rockies; major skiing territory.'

'So, the guy doesn't give a damn about his wife's addiction. He goes to Colorado and has a good time, while Karen Silvermann dries out in a clinic somewhere.' Connie tried to hang on to her and Kurt's version of events.

I saw another argument about to develop, until Dyanne Starr and Austin came over to join us.

'I want to thank you guys for coming to rehearsal today.' Miss Starr approached with a manic glint. She'd been hyper all morning, throwing her energy into the play with a 'show-must-go-on' attitude that was meant to increase our admiration for her.

It kind of did. But on the other hand, Starr never got rid of that 'look-at-me' trip either. Once a Broadway actress, always a performer. It came out in her reaction to Fiorello's murder the day before, with the moaning and the over-the-top tears. It was still there this morning; chin out, shoulders back, we-just-have-to-cowboy-up!

'No, really!' she insisted as we did the modest stuff.

'I'm proud of you guys; the way you're doing this for the school, hanging on in. And I guarantee you, we're gonna sock it to those audiences next week!'

Everything fell flat for a few seconds after this rousing speech. There were a couple of embarrassed coughs, then Austin with middle-aged spread came in with the observation that we were doing it for Mr Fiorello; for his memory, as a mark of respect.

No we're not! The thought never crossed my mind. Ditto Kate and Connie, I could tell by their faces. Which is another notch in my belt for the how-well-do-you-know-your-friends debate. I'd bet a million dollars they agreed with me on the respect-for-Fiorello score.

Miss Starr smiled at Austin, holding back the tears. 'You know Arnie Mercury took off in the middle of the night?' she informed us quietly. Like we were privileged to know this and mustn't spread it around.

'How do you mean, "took off"?' Kate said with a sharp edge.

Birdman Mercury, the messenger with wings on his boots. He spread them and flew.

'He loaded his bag into his pick-up truck and headed out of town.' The teacher swore it was the Bible truth. 'I guess it was the fact that the cops traced the murder weapon to his store-room.'

'Yeah, but that slaps you in the face a little too hard, don't you think?' Connie pointed out. 'Axe belongs to

42

Mercury, hence Mercury is the murderer!'

Miss Starr shrugged. 'Why else would he do a midnight runner?'

Because he's scared that it looks bad for him and he's not very bright, Kate and I thought. I swear she did from the look she gave me.

'But what would be his motive?' Austin inquired. Geek glasses pressed more firmly on to geek nose. What would be his motive? Exactly.

'Yeah!' Kate echoed. She was turning it into a personal issue against Miss Starr. 'Anyway, I heard he's a Christian, not the type who goes around with an axe.'

'Ouch!' Connie whispered to her as the teacher spotted a newcomer to the theatre. It was Mrs Fiorello, standing quietly at the door to the auditorium until someone finally noticed her. 'I hope she didn't hear that.'

'She looks . . . small!' I come out with stupid things like this.

I'd never taken much notice of the principal's wife, but it did suddenly strike me that she looked young and vulnerable. This came out as 'small'.

Miss Starr had gone right across to see what she wanted. I mean, under the circumstances it couldn't have been idle interest in next week's production.

'See that!' Connie hissed.

The two women were talking fast and furious. Mrs Fiorello looked like a moth beside Miss Starr's butterfly;

brown beside peacock blue, Miss Starr shaking her head, Mrs Fiorello quietly insisting on her point of view.

'Weird!' Connie breathed, her eyes alight with scandal. 'The widow and the mistress!'

I heard Kate swivel back to her sound-board and press keys like crazy. This was to stop herself from going, 'Wow, that's the first I heard! . . . Miss Starr and Fiorello? . . . Are you absolutely sure?'

She left all that stuff to me. Yes, Connie was one hundred per cent certain that the school principal had been having an affair with the drama teacher. It was common knowledge, and it was only dweebs like me who didn't know it.

'B-but . . . !' Dyanne Starr was a Fiorello fan, I had to admit. And, vice-versa, she could well be his type; shorter than him, curvy, with all that energy and charisma stuff. Except that would mean mousy little Mary Beth Fiorello definitely wasn't his type, yet he'd gone ahead and married her and had two kids . . .

Connie saw the confusion flicker in rapid waves across my face. She gave me a hard time. Did I remember when Starr went off to Fiorello's office to 'work on the letter to Don Silvermann'? Wasn't it obvious then?

'Not to me,' I admitted.

Connie laughed and turned to Kate. 'Get Joey,' she scoffed. Just like a guy. Did we go around with our eyes permanently shut, or what?

5

Teachers fall into the same category as parents in that you don't like to picture them in the sack with anybody. I mean, it's indecent. Ok, so I'm politically incorrect.

But that's why I never figured out Dyanne Starr and Fiorello until Connie enlightened us. Of course, all the signs had been there, it's just that I never bothered to read them.

'This is a whole different ball game,' Joey admitted. 'No more Mr Goody-Two-Shoes Fiorello.'

After rehearsal, we'd adjourned to the coffee bar in the Barnes and Noble bookshop off Fortune Park; me, Carter, Connie and Austin (Superglue) Wainwright.

'Why is it such a big deal?' Connie made out that everyone had affairs and that Carter being shocked was simply naive. 'Apart from the fact that Fiorello could hardly be seen as a babe magnet. Which makes his ability to score with Miss Starr a little surprising, I admit.'

'Women are attracted to guys with power,' Austin announced, straight from the psychology class he'd probably attended last week. 'They overlook their physical shortcomings in order to be seen with someone who has corporate muscle; hence Fiorello and Starr.'

'Shut up, Austin!' Connie said.

'So why would Mrs Fiorello want to come to rehearsal and talk with the mistress?' Joey had already blown his cool, so he plunged on with the next question for relationship expert Connie. 'Wouldn't she want to cut her dead forever now that her husband's . . . gone? Hey, maybe she didn't know about the affair?'

'She knew,' I said quietly, reading the signs in retrospect. For example, she'd made a point of asking me how Dyanne Starr had reacted to the news of Fiorello's murder. In fact, come to think about it, that was probably the sole reason for her visit to my house after she'd been to the mortuary.

'Yeah. You want my guess?' Connie would give it to us anyway. She was holding court in the murder-mystery section of the bookstore, surrounded by novels with lurid, bloodthirsty covers. 'I reckon Mrs Fiorello was telling Starr to stay away from the funeral! No way would she want the Other Woman weeping and wailing over the casket.'

I took a while to digest this one, then nodded.

'No,' Austin argued calmly.

(How were these two ever going to portray the tender farewell between Mr and Mrs Willy Loman in the final tragic scenes, when it was clear they hated each other's guts?)

'What do you mean, "no", Austin?' Connie's counter challenge came with an exasperated sigh.

So we were into a full-scale argument here.

Austin raised his voice. 'I mean, Connie, that you're dead wrong about the topic of conversation between Mary Beth Fiorello and Dyanne Starr. It had nothing to do with arrangements for the principal's funeral!'

'Shut up, Austin!' Connie turned her back.

'It had to do with a five thousand dollar reward.' He enjoyed delivering that one and sitting back to watch its impact.

I glanced at Carter and saw that he was too jumpy to sit around the low table scattered with crime books. He got up and paced the floor, listening hard. Austin's news made me nervous too. But, like Joey, I stayed quiet.

Connie's reaction came in late, after she'd coped with her surprise. 'Yeah, like you know everything, Austin!'

'I know about the reward. A cool five thousand for information leading to the arrest and conviction of Mr Fiorello's killer.'

Swivelling in her chair, Connie turned to Carter and me. 'Did you hear about this?'

We shook our heads.

Know-it-all Austin milked it for all it was worth. 'Try opening your ears some time, and you'd pick up the fact that Mrs Fiorello went to her minister to pray. The minister heard God's voice telling her to offer a reward.'

'No way!' Connie was openly gobsmacked.

'Believe me. The idea is to appeal to people's greed instead of letting the cops take forever to investigate using the normal route . . .'

'Yeah, yeah, Austin.' Carter broke his silence. 'We all know what a reward is for. God didn't give the minister the name of the guilty party by any chance?'

The thing about Austin is that he takes you literally (no sense of irony). 'Not the way I heard it,' he replied. 'But I do have my own suspicions.'

'Uh-oh, he has his suspicions!' Connie mocked.

Since he was in the right, Austin found it easy to brush off her mockery. He went on to tick off names on his fingers. 'Arnie Mercury; he was the one who indirectly brought the corpse to the cops' attention – so forget him. Mary Beth Fiorello; driven to it by insane jealousy – nope, too small to wield the axe. Three – and this is a distinct possibility here – a kid with a grudge who decides to commit a hate crime; the quiet type, the secret psychopath . . .'

'Someone like you, Austin?' Connie delivered her killer line with total disdain.

I didn't like the significant pause, or the way Austin's voice contained a jeering note as he outstared Connie.

'If you ask me, number three is the best option,' he went on. 'And if you ask me another question, like, who might this kid with a grudge be, I'd give you a name and that name would be Kurt Silvermann!'

'Shut up, Austin!' Connie, Carter and I said in unison.

But he did us a favour as a matter of fact, because it was that Silver-did-it moment in the bookshop that crystallised in my mind the fact that me and Joey would have to fight hard from now on to clear Kurt's name.

Carter agreed.

'Someone like Austin Wainwright,' he said, 'is jealous as hell of a kid like Kurt.'

It was only a short distance across the park from Barnes and Noble to the Roosevelt Building. Carter and I had split from Connie and Austin and come to the same conclusion: that we must above all try to find out where Kurt was hanging out. Until we knew where he was and got his version of the story of the last few days, there was very little we could do to help.

'Austin is a poisonous little toad,' I replied. Real cool and rational.

'If he goes around naming Kurt like that, the cops are gonna pick it up and pay it serious attention.' Carter walks fast when he's thinking hard, long legs covering the ground. He ducks his head and stares at a spot just in front of his feet; watch out old ladies and small kids!

'Austin's dead!' I vowed. Gone was all that stuff about not really knowing your friends. It just took Superglue, hanging round where he wasn't wanted, putting the suspicion about Kurt into sticky, oozing, jealousy-fed words for me to be convinced our guy was wholly innocent.

Gut reaction. Instinct. Intuition. Call it what you like.

'We gotta find Kurt and tell him to talk to the cops before they come down hard on him!' Joey said. 'If we go to the apartment and he's not home, we leave a message with his folks for him to get in touch.'

The elegant, white and silver building towered over the edge of the park, reminding you of ocean liners from the nineteen twenties. It came to a point like the prow of a ship; *Titanic*, Leonardo and Kate, ploughing on towards the green lawns, backed by billowing clouds.

'What if Kurt hasn't contacted his parents since Wednesday either? No, forget that. His dad knows about the exclusion.' There was the message on the principal's machine. 'But OK, what if his dad's so mad at him, Kurt's grounded and he won't let us see him?' I'd never met Mr Silvermann in person, so I had no idea what to expect.

'No way can he stop us if Kurt's here,' Joey insisted, striding through the subway, up the steps, across the sidewalk and through the plate glass entrance of the Roosevelt Building.

Still keep in mind ocean liners: polished metal, geometric friezes of inlaid wood, black marble floors. The bell-hops wear grey uniforms with gold braid; they open the doors for you to sail through.

Roosevelt is unique in Fortune City. It survived redevelopment so many times, it has more lives than a cat. That's because Big Money has always owned these apartments. So not even the solid silver Art Deco door handles have been replaced, and it's the original elevator that takes you up to the ninth floor.

Or would, if the snotty bell-hops didn't try to prevent you.

'Don't I know you?' Cheesy grin as the Braided One stepped across Joey's path.

'No way, man.' Carter reached this way then that, trying to press the elevator button.

'Yeah, you were here a couple of days back.' He looked me up and down, stirring it. 'Different girl.'

'So?' Sullen Carter gave up on the elevator and headed for the marble stairs, only to be intercepted again.

'So, if you came to see the Silvermanns, I got orders not to let anybody go up.'

51

The guy was all of two years older than us, acned, overweight; pretty unattractive, actually.

'So throw me in gaol,' Joey muttered, ducking past the bell-hop.

We could both outrun him up nine flights of stairs, and he knew it.

Bell-boy returned to his cubicle by the main door and no doubt called the Silvermanns while Joey and I went right on up.

Don Silvermann was waiting for us.

He smiled and said hi and invited us in.

What was this? Why wasn't he Big Bad Daddy?

'Kurt always talks about you,' he told Joey. 'And – the guy who's a good ball player?'

'Ziggy,' Carter informed him politely.

We were inside the apartment. There was genuine Japanese, hand-painted silk on the walls, cream rugs on the polished wood floors. A fake log-fire burned in the English-style Adam fireplace; the gold-framed mirror above was in fact a wide-screen TV. Oh, and there was serious Art on the panelled walls.

'Yeah; Ziggy,' Mr Silvermann chuckled. 'From what I hear, he's a talented guy.'

'Is Kurt here?' I asked. I'd just read the name Georgia O'Keefe in the bottom corner of a close-up painting of a pink flower. We were talking hundreds of thousands of dollars. My mom would've killed to get her hands on that picture.

'No, he's not actually,' Kurt's father said, hands in the pockets of his dark blue trousers. He favoured bold coloured sweaters with diamond patterns, apparently. They highlighted his all-year tan and complemented his swept-back, silver hair. Golf pro hanging out at the clubhouse; you get the picture.

'Er, we need to see him,' Carter volunteered.

From the mumbling way Joey spoke and the fact that I was feeling overawed by the money on the walls alone, I knew Silvermann was going to give us the run around, no problem.

'I need to see him too,' he laughed, tapping the surface of the walnut bureau close to where I stood. Expensive aftershave wafted up my nostrils. 'I just flew in from Colorado to a note from his school principal telling me my son has been excluded for non-attendance and requesting an interview with me on Monday morning!'

I coughed and swallowed hard. Rewind. Did I just dream all that stuff about the axe and the corpse? Or was Don Silvermann seriously behind the times?

Hey, no. He was the one who had called Fiorello to fix a time. I glanced at the desk, but Mr Silvermann made sure to whisk away the letter on school headed notepaper. He left behind the stub of an airline ticket which read first class return, Fortune City to New York JFK. The return section was dated three days ago; Wednesday 28th November.

'Lucky for Kurt, his mom doesn't know about this yet,' Don Silvermann went on, still apparently amused, bemused, at a loss as to what to do over his wayward son. 'She wanted to extend her skiing trip, so she stayed on in Boulder. Leaving me, as it happens, to face the music on Monday with Mr – er?' He looked to Carter for more help with names.

'Fiorello,' Joey mumbled. 'Excuse me, sir; didn't you hear the news?'

'I heard the Dow Jones gained twenty points,' Kurt's father quipped. Money joke. Finance. Ha-ha.

When Carter broke it to him, minus the blood on the walls and other details, including the fact that he and I had been there when the body was discovered and that Kurt's name was in the picture as a suspect, Mr Silvermann seemed genuinely shocked.

'Oh my God, that's awful! Did they arrest someone yet? Did they work out a motive?'

'All fake!' I gave Carter my opinion on the train over to Connie's place in East Village to tell her that we'd picked up precisely no useful information regarding Kurt from his ever-loving father.

'So why would he lie?' Joey sat by the window,

looking down on the wet, tree-lined streets. A siren wailed and an ambulance sped by.

'I don't know why. I just know he did.' About flying in from Colorado, about not knowing until today that Kurt had been excluded. Probably about a whole lot of other important stuff, like the whereabouts of his wife and son. 'You wanna know something? I wouldn't trust that guy further than I could throw him.'

Carter stared at the raindrops hitting the windowpane and trickling down. 'This is really getting to me,' he admitted. 'I want the cops to do something. I want them to find a crazy guy sleeping in his pick-up in a supermarket car lot, covered in Fiorello's blood. He's so out of it, he doesn't even know what he did. They arrest him and stick him in a secure hospital. End of story.'

I shook my head, slipped my hand through the crook of his arm. 'Sorry, Joey, that's not about to happen.'

'I don't want it to be someone we know,' he insisted. 'Not even Arnie Mercury, poor sucker.'

Our visit to Connie's house coincided with the early evening news bulletin, which we had to listen to through music from upstairs, a Disney movie on the TV in her kid sister's room and a running battle between another sister and her mom.

'. . . Why can't I sleep over at Heidi's place?'

'Because Heidi's mom ain't gonna be there, and you're only eleven years old, for Christ's sake!'

'Is this the local station?' Fighting the noise level, Connie flicked channels to check she was tuned into the city news. 'Yeah, this is it. Kate, Carter, move out of the way, will you? This could be important.'

A strike by drivers on the Circle Train was planned for the three Saturdays before Christmas. Mel Gibson was in town to promote a movie. Police had made a breakthrough in the murder investigation involving Fortune City High principal, John Fiorello.

'See!' Connie cried. 'Mom, keep it down, why can't you? I'm trying to listen to the News here!'

'. . . But why can't I sleep over at Heidi's?'

'I told you why already. Try closing the door, Connie, if it's not too much effort to get up off of your ass!'

I closed the door for her, so we could concentrate on the reporter standing in the rain outside our school entrance, talking to camera.

'Yes, Matthew, there has been a significant development in this investigation. Late this afternoon, the police called a news conference to tell journalists that they had in fact identified the type of shoe most probably worn by the killer in this brutal, apparently motiveless incident.'

Matthew, back in the studio, fired off the necessary,

predictable question. 'And they were able to do this by examining the bloody footprints inside the murder room?'

'That's right,' the rain-spattered reporter confirmed. 'Now the interesting thing, Matthew, is that this was an unusual print; the tread was matched up with a specialist sports boot worn by rock climbers and other extreme sport enthusiasts.'

My heart missed a beat right then and there; I don't know about Carter and Connie.

'That kind of narrows things down, Tammy.' The newsreader led into his final question. 'So did you learn anything more specific?'

Tammy smiled. 'We did, Matthew. Police investigations on this issue of the specialist shoe led them to all the major sports retailers in Fortune City, many of whom keep comprehensive records on their customers: credit card numbers, names, occasionally even shoe size.' The camera went in close, picked up the excitement in the reporter's violet blue eyes.

We all guessed the next bit, before Lois Lane, girl reporter, spelled it out. The room was deathly quiet except for her voice.

'The result of this intensive research is that detectives were able to pinpoint a name, which they refuse to make public at this stage of their investigation. All they would confirm is that they're now actively seeking a former pupil of the school, an extreme sports fanatic who hasn't been seen since Wednesday.'

Connie clamped her hands up to her face and shook her head frantically. I clawed on the sofa to grab the remote and turn off the TV.

But not before Tammy signed off with her dramatic revelation. 'And, Matthew, the hot news on the street is that the unnamed suspect belongs to a prominent and wealthy Fortune City family. That's all I can say right now except, watch this space!'

Click. The screen went blank.

Connie went hysterical.

So much for the crazy guy sleeping in the pick-up. So much for the random, motiveless paranoid schizophrenic. The cops had just made Kurt their official prime suspect.

6

Personally, I would cancel the show.

The principal was dead, the cops were still crawling all over the school building, one cast member (namely Connie) was finding it increasingly hard to hold it together on account of her would-be boyfriend being currently missing and a suspect in a major homicide investigation.

I gave Kate my theory: that it would be more respectful and easier on us all if *Death of a Salesman* bit the dust.

But Starr, with a martyr's glow lighting up her face, said we had to continue.

'Mr Fiorello – John – would've wanted it this way,' she told us as we gathered on Sunday morning for the final dress rehearsal. The production was due to run Monday through Thursday. This was our last chance for a full rehearsal.

'I can't do this. It's too hard.' Connie looked like she hadn't slept for worrying about Kurt. Tears kept welling up and sliding down her cheeks.

Miss Starr thought she understood, but didn't. 'I know; it's gonna take everything we've got. But, Connie, try not to think about what's taken place. It happened. There's not a thing we can do, except concentrate on the future and try to fulfil what we know would make John happy and proud of each and every one of us.'

I reckon Starr missed her vocation. She should write speeches for the president's office. With a skill like that, she could whitewash any crime and misdemeanour a politician might care to commit.

She could also gloss over the fact that we all now knew about the secret affair. No one said so, but it was in the ether; people were looking at her differently, whispering a little behind her back. But it didn't seem to bother her; maybe the opposite. Dyanne Starr likes to be centre stage, which is where being the mistress put her.

Just as long as the finger of suspicion, currently pointing at Kurt Silvermann, didn't swing her way.

Starr took Connie by the hand. 'C'mon, try!'

Connie sighed and nodded. Then she went to change into her mousy Mrs Loman costume. Meanwhile, Starr coached Austin for the scene, early on, when we learn he had a woman in a hotel room for whom he bought nylons instead of paying instalments on the car. Yeah, Willy Loman cheated on his wife too.

'What're you thinking?' Kate sat at her sound-board sipping coffee from a plastic cup.

We'd reached the end of Act One, and Starr was up onstage, going crazy with the kid playing Biff. 'You bring the whole production down with that attitude, Stephen! It's like you don't care! What happened to your commitment to the group?'

I killed the lights. 'Nothing,' I told Kate.

'Impossible. You can't think nothing.'

I glanced at her; risky because if I'm sitting close to her and I see the way her dark lashes curl and strands of hair fall across her cheek, I always want to touch her. So I sat on my hands, just in case. 'OK, I was thinking about Arnie.'

'What about him?'

'I saw him on my way here. He was on the train over from Marytown, heading for church.'

Tiny frown lines appeared between Kate's eyebrows. 'Didn't we hear he disappeared?'

I nodded. 'Yeah. But the poor guy's not even very good at that. I got talking to him. He said he didn't drive out of town like Starr told us. He went to his brother's house on Thirty-second Street, which was naturally the first place the cops came looking for him.'

'Why do you say "poor guy" like that?' Kate slid the base of her coffee cup along the edge of the sound console, back and forth, making the contents rock.

'Because he doesn't know what hit him,' I explained. 'Here he is, doing a job. It's not a great job, opening doors, counting tables and chairs, supervising the standard of campus cleanliness, but Arnie's had worse.'

'You talked to him at length?' She put down the cup

and swivelled on her stool to face me.

I nodded. 'He opened up to me. Like he said, there he was, doing no harm, going about his business. Then he finds a corpse.'

'*We* find a corpse,' she corrected me.

'Exactly. We were in on the discovery, but you notice it's Arnie the cops give a hard time to.'

'What kind of hard time?'

'They ask him over and over again about the axe. How come it was the one embedded in the principal's door? How did it get from Arnie's store-room to the scene of the killing? He tells them he has no idea.'

'Don't they believe him?

'Arnie doesn't think so. He told me he only went to Marty, his brother's, to get a break. But the cops acted like this proved he was guilty of Murder One!'

'Yeah, I wonder why?' Keeping her eye on Starr, who was still laying into the cast over their shortcomings, Kate was listening hard. 'What makes them do that?'

I remembered asking Arnie himself the same question. Sitting there on the train as it came into a station, he'd looked like he hardly knew where he was. He twitched and picked at a piece of cotton thread on his jacket. 'The cops know I got a conviction back in the eighties,' he told me quietly.

I asked him what the conviction was for.

Homicide was the answer.

I explained the situation to Kate now; the reason why Arnie Mercury became the sad, scared, silent guy he was. 'He aided a suicide,' I told her. 'His mother was sick with cancer. Arnie was the one who did what she asked, which was to give her a fatal dose of morphine. Technically that's homicide in the state where he lived. He went to gaol for five years.'

She didn't ask me any more questions after that.

I recalled how Arnie's voice broke as he went through the reasons why the cops wouldn't give it a rest. And how he recognised the handle of the axe as it crashed through the door panel, and knew right then that it would put him at the top of the list of suspects.

'But it didn't,' I tried to reason with him. 'They put out a news bulletin that they're looking for someone else who was wearing a particular type of shoe.' I didn't name the name that had sent Connie crazy. 'Didn't you hear?'

Arnie shook his head. I don't think this got through, even after I explained it more. He was too fixated on the reward he'd heard about; the one Mrs Fiorello put up. 'I don't know why she did that,' he said a couple of times. 'Why did she have to put up the five thousand?'

'I don't know, Arnie.' By this time I was speaking slowly, like you do to a young kid. 'I guess it's something you do if you're desperate.'

'But Mary Beth didn't have to do that. God will punish the killer in His own way.'

I was glad then that my stop had come. I didn't want to get into the God stuff and the glazed looks. I stood up from my seat, swayed, grabbed the overhead strap. 'Take care, Arnie,' I said as I left the train. I told him, try not to worry. Hah!

So Sunday was the day for confessions. Not mine; other people's.

First there was Arnie, poor guy.

Then Starr chose after the rehearsal to have a major breakdown, and she picked me to have it in front of.

What is it about me? Is it the fact that I limit what I say to what's strictly necessary, thus giving the other guy the space to spill his guts?

Well, let me tell it for the record: there's only one person I want to have a one to one with, and her name isn't Dyanne Starr.

'. . . I'm sorry!' the drama teacher sobbed. The others had already left the building, including Kate, who had gone to be with Connie at her place. I was doing the site supervisor's job of checking that the doors and windows were locked. I came across Starr standing like a zombie in the corridor outside the principal's office. The second she saw me, she started to cry and apologise.

Of my two options, to walk away in embarrassment or to stand there until she stopped, I unwisely chose the latter.

Crying for Miss Starr was a big deal. For a start, it was noisy, then there was mascara, snot, the full orchestra. 'I don't have a Kleenex,' I mumbled, fumbling in my empty pockets.

'Oh, Joey, I'm sorry. I'll be fine soon. Just give me a minute!' She smudged at the mascara and drew deep, shuddering breaths, hair drooping over her temples, mouth turned down at the corners like a Greek tragic mask.

'Miss Starr!' I begged. Did you touch her, put an arm around her to help her control herself? Why didn't someone write a rule book to cover this?

Luckily, she stiffened and backed off as I approached. 'No, Joey; don't be kind to me. It only makes me worse!'

Right. I made a note of that.

'I didn't want anyone to see me like this. I'm trying so hard to get through without falling apart, but it was walking by the room . . . it, it sort of got to me!'

'I'm sorry,' I murmured, setting off the tears again.

'No, I'm OK!' Up went the hand to warn me off. 'You know the worst part? It's not being able to say how I feel. I mean, you know, everyone looks at Mary Beth and says how terrible, what can we do? But someone like me; they don't know how to handle it. So they fall back on the fact that John and I were colleagues and give me the official line. So sorry, such a brilliant principal, what a loss to the school.'

I nodded in the right places, I hoped.

'You're sweet, Joey. I can talk to you.'

No, you can't. I'm a student, you're on staff. Remember the protocol!

Miss Starr was no mind reader. 'Deep down, I'm devastated,' she confessed. 'I've realised how much I depended on him being there for me, and I know in my heart that I'll never love anyone as much as I loved him.'

No! No! Press Delete. Help, Kate! Help, anybody!

'Can you believe he's dead?' Starr gasped.

'Miss Starr, come away from the door . . . please!'

She pushed me away and broke through the forensic tape across the entrance to Fiorello's office. Then she stood staring at the blood-stained walls.

She sagged, went quiet, then began again in a totally different mood. 'I wasn't the first,' she said softly, her back towards me, her fingers touching a gash on the desk where the axe had come down. 'And I wouldn't have been the last.'

This time, I went right up beside her, and she didn't move away.

'John was – what would you call it? – a serial adulterer,' she told me. 'He made no secret of the fact to me. I tried to tell myself I was special; *the* one. But who was I fooling? Every girl thinks that, I guess.'

Jeez, no; this was too real. Dyanne Starr stripped bare, minus the acting and the ego. Poor woman. OK, I'm a soft touch, but truly I was feeling almost as sorry for her as I had for Arnie Mercury.

'The thing I couldn't get a handle on at first was Mary Beth,' she went on. 'What kept her in a marriage that was so rocky she had to hang on to the side to stay in the boat?'

I shrugged. *Don't look at me!*

'For a while I guessed it was the kids. Mary Beth stayed with John for the sake of the children. Then I thought maybe the comfortable salary. But no.'

'It's the Christian thing.' Even I could chip in with a suggestion here. To me this was obvious.

Miss Starr nodded. 'All this offering the other cheek stuff. I worked out Mary Beth was strong on martyrdom. And hot on the marriage vows; for better, for worse.'

There was a silence, a pause for thought that made the hairs on my neck stand on end.

'And why not?' Starr gave a bitter laugh. 'These people who have God in their lives don't go through the same tortures of self-doubt that the rest of us do!'

'Mrs Fiorello seems a pretty together person,' I agreed. We'd all heard how strong she'd been through everything, and determined to catch the guilty party. And Kate had told me she was calm when she came to her house.

'More than that.' Miss Starr backed out of the room. 'She's the sort of woman a man never leaves.'

Yeah; together. Dependable, a mother, reasonably good looking in her own way.

Now, the big question is, did the comment Miss Starr made next come out of jealousy, guilt and all the deep stuff she was feeling right then? Or was she hinting at a whole bunch of things I knew nothing about?

'Mary Beth Fiorello has the most willpower of any person I ever knew,' she confided. 'She can twist people around her litle finger, make them do anything she wants them to do.'

'Hey!' I protested. This seemed kind of – blasphemous. Was that the word?

There wasn't a trace of a tear in Starr's eyes now. She looked clear at me. 'Believe me, this woman is not what she seems!'

My last job before I left, having taken confession from Miss Starr, was to return the site keys to the superintendent's office.

Jeez, would I be glad to be out of there, joining Kate and Connie on the Kurt trail, which is what we'd planned to carry on doing.

('Kurt didn't do it!' Connie insisted. 'Whatever they say, he was *not* the one!'

'We believe you,' Kate tried to tell her. 'It's not us you have to convince.'

Kate really cares about her friends. To my mind, that's a big plus factor.)

I was walking down the stone steps towards Arnie's basement office. (Arnie by this time being suspended pending investigations.) I had Kate on my mind; so what's new? The door to the superintendent's store-room was open on my left as I passed by.

I hang the keys on the hook inside the office. I note that Arnie keeps a tidy desk; mouse on the mouse-pad, yellow post-it notes in a neat row on the side of the monitor. Regret the fact once more that the guy is going through a rough time.

Remind myself to look him up after school tomorrow, to see how he's getting along.

Turn, retrace my steps. Glance to my right into the dim store-room.

I see a pair of legs dangling, think, *That's not right*.

Enter, see a scarecrow body hanging by a rope.

Know that the neck is broken and that I'm too late.

I cut this back to the bare facts; it's tough to dwell on.

Some time between getting off the train to go to church earlier that morning and the time I returned the keys, Arnie Mercury had taken a rope from a metal trunk by the door of his store-room, slung it over a steel beam, made a noose, climbed on a chair, kicked it away and hanged himself.

7

'What happened to Joey?' Connie looked at her watch, immune to the babble of noise going on around us.

('Mom, can Heidi come play? Can she bring her Barbies?'

'No, I already told you, we're going to a movie.'

'But, Mom!'

Upstairs, loud TV. Outside on the stoop, kids with ghetto blasters.)

'Joey said he'd be here,' I insisted. But even I was getting worried. How long could locking doors and returning the keys take?

'That was an hour ago. Listen, Kate, I can't stomach doing nothing. Kurt needs help, and here we are sitting on our butts!'

The door burst open. Connie's kid sister, Courtney, burst into the room, grabbed nine inches of naked, blonde-maned plastic doll from the coffee table and raced out again.

'I'm thinking!' I told Connie. 'About this evidence of the footprints on the carpet in Fiorello's room, and the link with Kurt. How did that come about?'

She stood up to confront me. 'Yeah, sure, go ahead, accuse him right out. Claim the five grand, why don't you?'

'I never said Kurt was guilty! What I said was, we need to work out the problem about the shoe prints. There has to be some other explanation . . .'

Connie cut me short. 'So ask him.'

I laughed. 'Oh sure!'

'I mean it, Kate. I can take you to him right this minute if you want me to!'

'B–but – you know where he is?'

She gave me a defiant look and didn't answer directly. 'You want to talk footprints? So come with me!'

We didn't wait any longer for Joey. No, we left Connie's place and got right on the train to the centre of town, stepped off again at the City Hospital station.

I'd tried the recriminations – 'Why didn't you tell me? I'm your friend. You could've trusted me!' – and got nowhere.

All Connie would say was she promised Kurt that she wouldn't say a word.

'So what changed your mind?' I asked as we negotiated the crossings and headed down the side of the hospital building.

Connie paused, her hand on the buzzer that would gain us entrance to a semi-basement lobby under the street level plastic surgery department. 'Did you ever try keeping a secret as big as this?' she asked me. 'The cops are looking for Kurt on a murder charge, and I'm the only one in Fortune City who knows where he's holed up. That's some responsibility!'

'Yeah.' I stared up at thirty floors of concrete and glass. *Thanks, Connie, for dumping this one on me!* Only, I understood what she was saying; a problem like this was something she needed to share.

'I tell you, Kate, I reached the point when I couldn't think straight. I need you to talk to Kurt because he's not listening to me. Only, you have to promise not to say a word to anybody, OK?'

'Not even Joey?'

Finger still on the buzzer, Connie hesitated. 'I guess that'll be up to Kurt; if he doesn't blow me out when he sees I brought you, that is.'

So I was far from happy when she finally pressed the button and spoke into the intercom.

'Kurt, it's me, Connie.'

There was a click, she pushed the glass door open and we went inside.

'What is this place?' I read plates on doors as we walked through the lobby and down the empty corridor: the name of a natural childbirth trust, then a cancer research organisation, and other less well known charities as we went along.

'Offices,' Connie told me. 'It's OK, there's no one around today; it's Sunday.'

I nodded and glanced through open doors to see printers and photocopiers standing silent. Everything was orderly: filing cabinets, telephones, banks of computers.

Connie found time for explanations as we headed for the far end of the corridor. 'Kurt's mom is a major figure in Childscape; you know, the charity working to keep kids off the streets and out of the care system?'

'I never knew that.' Karen Silvermann got her face into society magazines for attending high-class parties, but I hadn't seen any mention of charity work. Though I did know there was a type of wealthy woman up and down the land who met for lunch and planned good works of the pop-concert fund-raising variety.

'She works hard at it,' Connie insisted. 'It's a good cause. Anyway, it was Kurt's idea to hole up in Childscape's office because he knew it was closed for refurbishment. They had a flood last month, which wrecked all the equipment. Childscape workers moved out to an empty room up the corridor, leaving Kurt an opportunity of grabbing somewhere where no one would think to look.'

'He had a key?' I asked.

'I guess. Look, I know what you're thinking – why would he then risk everything by contacting me?'

'No, actually.' Connie's question came further down my list. 'I was wondering what he ran away from in the first place!'

'Kate's cool. She'll help. Trust me, Kurt!'

I was standing by the door of the Childscape office, watching two very scared people.

Connie had pleaded with Kurt not to blame her for bringing me on to the scene. 'I was going crazy keeping it to myself, then I heard the news broadcast last night!'

'You should've checked it out with me!' Kurt kept glancing my way, pulling Connie further into the corner to try to get out of earshot.

'Yeah, then you'd have told me, no way!' Tears streamed down Connie's face as she tugged her arms free.

'You bet your life! The more people find out about this place, the more I'm in schtuck!'

Unreal. I was the unwelcome third party hovering by the door of a ruined office; paint peeling off the walls, carpet tiles curling and lifting off the floor, a door into an inner room still running with water from a trickling overhead pipe. Two of my best friends were ripping each other to shreds over stuff to do with trust and betrayal.

'It's done, so why not forget it?' I pointed out to Kurt. 'Connie had had enough; she couldn't take any more; period.'

He frowned and hung his head. 'Yeah, sorry, Con.'

'It's OK.' She dried her eyes. 'Thanks, Kate.'

'That's OK.'

We were dancing around each others' finer feelings without getting to the nitty gritty. I should say that Kurt looked less godlike than when I last saw him. Shadows had darkened under his eyes, his chin had grown stubble. He needed a shower, then lots of sleep.

'So what happened?' I asked.

'You mean, why am I here?' He half sat, half leaned against a table stacked with trash bins, flood-damaged books, a coffee-maker. 'If I said it has nothing to do with what happened to Fiorello, would you believe me?'

'Yes.' No doubt. I wanted him to know that.

Staring at me, he nodded slowly. 'OK, it's family stuff – major problems with my dad.'

Don Silvermann with the monogrammed golf sweaters and the stick-on smile. 'You called him and told him you were excluded?'

'I didn't have to. He flew home early and was there to meet me when I touched base, Wednesday afternoon.'

My turn to frown. I was intrigued. 'That's not what he said on Fiorello's answer machine. Nor what he told Carter and me when we called in at your place yesterday.'

'He gave you the ski-trip story?' Kurt guessed. 'And

I bet he bribed the bell-hop to follow the party line too. You want to know what my father was really doing this past week?'

'It would help.' To stop my head from whirling with questions that found no answers. I was beginning to feel uncomfortable in this airless, windowless room. Kurt let a pregnant pause develop into a significant silence, then socked me the unexpected truth.

'He was busy getting my mom certified as unfit to administer her own affairs. Isn't that what they call it; the official version of crazy?'

Get this; there was no slaloming off-piste, only the dizzy heights of deception and the pit of betrayal.

Put more simply, the Silvermanns had been nowhere near Boulder, Colorado, but in New York. Dear Don had booked Karen into a drying-out clinic for serious alcoholics who need guaranteed privacy and who have enough dough to pay for it. Not for the first time, Kurt's mom had reached a level of desperation over her drinking that called for hospitalisation.

'She's been a fully subscribed member of Alcoholics Anonymous for years,' Kurt told me. 'Mostly it's under control, which means she can do good voluntary work for this charity, using her contacts to produce big donations and keeping dozens of kids off the streets. That's what she does with most of her life. Only sometimes, things at home would get so bad, she'd hit the bottle again.'

'In what way, bad?' I cut in. I imagined the answer must have something to do with silver-haired Don, and I was right.

'My dad. He's not how he comes across in public, with the stockbroker suits and the golfing buddies and such like. In the home he's real heavy.'

'Violent,' Connie added. 'He gets off on beating his kids. The guy should be in gaol for child abuse.'

I pictured the intimacy in the past weeks between her and Kurt which would've produced this revelation from him. Wow, these two were a serious item, I realised.

'My mom was always caught in the middle, trying to protect my sister Elouise and me. So she turned to alcohol as a way to help herself, and that was the beginning of the slide, and how come she ended up several times in the most expensive substance abuse clinic in New York.'

'Including this last week?' I was beginning to get the full depressing, painful picture. 'But what's this about him certifying her as crazy?'

'I'm getting there. All the money comes from her side of the family, right? The Silvermanns have the name, but they were never good at handling dough. So Dad finds himself a rich wife and he's happy.

'Only, he's a lousy husband and father, as it turns out, and Mom begins to say she'll get a divorce. He turns around and begs her to stay and patch up the marriage.' Kurt paused again, presumably to let a wave of bad memories wash over his head. 'This happens more times than Elouise and I can count. Until this last time, just before Mom hit the bottle, she really did go to her lawyer to start drawing up papers for the divorce. Which meant Dad had to act fast if he wanted to keep his hands on the homes, the cars, the paintings.

'So he finds himself a tame psychiatrist called Erskine Grainger who would be willing to put Mom through psychological tests while she's at the clinic. Then this guy would swing the test results to prove some kind of personality disorder which would mean that Mom wasn't competent to make decisions on her own behalf – I don't know exactly how they do that, but believe me, it happens – and, ker-ching! Dad signs all the cheques from now on and Mom doesn't have any rights left. Can you believe that?'

I nodded and grimaced. With millions at stake and a greedy, violent and basically immoral guy behind it, I believed it all right. 'Don't tell me he got away with it.'

Taking a deep breath, Kurt brought me up to date. 'My sister, Elouise; she visited Mom at the clinic on Tuesday and sussed out what was going on because one of the nurses let slip a few things about Dad's Dr

Grainger. Mom was too sedated and out of it to realise anything. Elouise panicked, called me Tuesday night and told me she was gonna check Mom out of the clinic first thing Wednesday, which she did.

'Major drama; Dad gets there thirty minutes too late to stop my sister rescuing my mom. They're gone; whereabouts unknown. Elouise hid her pretty good, I know that for a fact. The only thing Dad can do is get on a plane back to Fortune and try to force the information out of me.'

'Force?' I echoed. By now, the picture I had of Don Silvermann was pretty horrific. On top of which, Kurt's little local difficulty with the school principal was looking like chicken-feed.

'He's a big guy.' Kurt shrugged.

Connie stepped up beside him and slipped her hand into his.

'But I can handle him,' he assured us, only semi-convincingly.

I looked for bruises and cuts, saw a scrape across his knuckles, healed into a brown scab, a red mark on his cheekbone. 'Do you know where your mom is?' I asked.

He nodded. 'No way would I tell Dad, though. And I was out of there the first chance I got. I headed here to Mom's old office, hoping no one would find me.'

'Then he called me.' Connie still held his hand, looking kind of brave and proud. 'Yeah, sorry, Kate; I lied to you. I brought him food, a couple of blankets. That's it. The story so far!'

Not quite. On top of Kurt's ongoing family problems, there was one particularly brutal murder of an unpopular school principal.

A five thousand dollar reward.

And a pair of expensive climbing shoes.

'I need to know about the shoes,' I said, keeping the tension out of my voice as best I could. 'Connie told you they matched footprints at the scene with shoes you bought?'

Kurt nodded. His mouth twitched and he had problems meeting my gaze.

C'mon, Kurt, please! Give me something I can use!

'What can I say?' He raised his hands as if warding me off.

'Say you were nowhere near Fiorello's office!' Connie instructed; loyal, loud, imploring.

'I wasn't, OK!'

'The shoes, Kurt!' If he couldn't convince me, what chance did he have with a detective at headquarters when they eventually smoked him out of hiding?

'I don't know. Maybe someone wanted me in the frame, maybe they planted the evidence . . .'

'You've got to do better than that!' Even Austin Wainwright, who hated Kurt's guts, and other kids who might have reasons to be jealous, would hardly risk their own skin by going into a room where a murder had recently taken place simply to frame him.

'OK, so it's a coincidence! Someone else has the same shoes!' More desperate now, Kurt broke away from Connie and slammed the edge of the table.

'Look in my eyes and tell me that again,' I told him. I was only putting him under the kind of pressure the cops would eventually. And remember, I *wanted* to believe him.

Kurt whirled around from the table. 'You don't give up do you? Once you sink your fangs in . . . !'

'Kurt, it's not Kate's fault . . .' Connie saw what I was saying. She was scared for him, wanting the full truth and nothing but the truth as much as I did. 'What is it you're not telling us?'

'Oh Jesus!' He let his head drop and clutched his temples with both hands. When he looked up and spoke to Connie, there were tears in his eyes. 'How did the cops learn I owned the climbing shoes?' he asked, his voice breaking into a hoarse whisper.

'They checked the sportswear stores, came up with store card details.' Connie looked to me for confirmation.

I nodded.

'They'd better double check.'

She frowned. 'For what, Kurt?'

He blinked and let the tears slide down his cheeks. 'You remember I told you about the trip to the Rockies in the Christmas vacation? Me and my dad are meeting up with his buddies to go climbing. Macho bonding stuff; Dad's big on that.'

'Yeah, I remember,' Connie whispered.

'So I went to the store to buy shoes. Then I took them home to show Dad. You see what I'm saying?'

She steeled herself to look into his eyes. 'No!'

But I did.

'Dad went in later to buy some, get it?'

Connie's eyes widened and she clutched both his arms. 'The identical style?'

'Right! It'll show up on the store card: one pair, size eleven, for me; one pair, size twelve, for Dad!'

8

'I don't have long to live, and it's better that way.' I picked up the suicide note on Arnie's super-organised desk, after I'd dialled emergency services and told them what had taken place. Reading the note was a way of avoiding going back into the store-room. Red alert: hanging man in there, me too terrified to go anywhere near it.

'God doesn't want me to go on. I hear what he tells me; that I don't deserve to remain in this world after what I did.'

The guy was hearing voices, for Christ's sake! There was no crazy bum sleeping rough in a pick-up; there was only Arnie after all.

'Before I go, I want to say sorry to a few people. Sorry to my mom, if what I did all those years ago was wrong. I did it to ease her pain. Sorry to my brother, for bringing more hurt to the family. Ron, it's best this way. Try and forget about me, have a nice life.'

I was cracking up reading the uneven writing, the letters slanting backwards and forwards, missing the line on the flower-bordered notepaper. My hand shook, my vision blurred. How wrong could you be? Arnie's axe.

Arnie raising the blade above Fiorello's head, bringing it crashing down . . . The simple answer staring me in the face, and I'd said, no way, not Arnie; it must be some other blood-crazed maniac out there.

Confession time. Roses around the edge of the pink page, sitting down at his desk with a noose and a convenient beam in mind, writing out a last desperate plea for forgiveness.

I read the final paragraph. 'Sorry, Mary Beth, if I caused you pain. I believed at the time I was right, just like with Mom. But there's a grief in my heart now, a sorrow in my soul. God says, "It's time." He's calling and I must heed that call. I ask you to forgive me. God bless you and Krystal and Nathan. That's all. Arnie.'

Though the cops took the note and went through everything thoroughly – certifying approximate time of death as 11 am, manner of death as asphyxiation due to hanging, taking Arnie away in a body bag – I still felt I owed it to him to go see Mrs Fiorello.

There wasn't a clear reason, more a feeling that being the first to read the note had turned me into some kind of messenger between them. I wanted to reinforce the poor guy's apology by giving it to her by word of mouth, knowing that it might not be high on the cops' list of things to do.

I did stop to ask myself why I was still thinking

of Arnie as 'poor guy' since I learned he was the one who wielded the axe. A picture of him twitching and pecking at life like a scared bird flashed into my head. Black and glossy and beaky, *peck-peck*. Silent. *Peck*. Confused.

'You OK?' one cop had asked me. He recognised me from the situation on Friday, said how unlucky could you get, and I'd better hope things didn't run in threes. Thanks, sergeant. Another corpse, and I'd be running to see a shrink.

I'd told him I was fine. He'd said I'd done everything right; leaving stuff as I found it, not touching anything.

I'd said as a matter of fact I'd read the note. My prints would be on it.

'Don't worry. We'll eliminate you from our inquiries!' Small joke, friendly grin. 'In fact, this little scene just about wraps the whole thing up, wouldn't you say?'

I'd asked him why Arnie might have killed Fiorello.

The grin had turned cynical. 'You want a motive as well?'

No, maybe not. Maybe a confession was as good as it got.

But still, I had in my mind the loose end of Mary Beth Fiorello. So I stepped on the train for Constitution Square, wondering, would she and the kids be home?

Krystal Fiorello opened the door to me like any eight-year-old kid wary of strangers. She had a mass of wavy, dark hair the same colour as Mary Beth's, but not tamed into any style, and the same oval face, not yet schooled to be expressionless. She stared resentfully at me through a six inch crack in the door, keeping the safety chain securely fastened.

'Is your mom home from church?' I asked.

'We didn't go to church.'

'So she's here?'

'Who's asking?' The big, light brown eyes looked angry and suspicious. I guess that's natural when your family takes a terrific shock like losing a parent.

'Could you tell her it's Joey Carter, please?'

'She can't see you right now. She's taking a phone call,' came the well-rehearsed reply. No way was the kid prepared to let me set foot inside the house.

In any case, I was changing my mind; maybe it would be best if I didn't intrude.

'. . . That's OK, honey; I just came off the phone.' Mary Beth Fiorello appeared just as I was about to turn away. She unhitched the safety chain and opened the door wide, dressed in a loose white shirt and black trousers, and wearing a black band in her hair which kept the curls back from her face. Already several steps ahead of me, she insisted that I stay.

'No, really . . .' I was backing off. 'You have stuff to do, I'll come back some other time.'

'Joey, come in. Listen, if it's about Arnie; I just spoke to the police.'

So at least I didn't have to break the news. 'I'm sorry,' I mumbled. I took in books on shelves lining the hall, soft, rich rugs, a quiet, orderly atmosphere.

But Mrs Fiorello herself wasn't as calm as I'd seen her up till now. She was uptight, rounding up Krystal towards the playroom where I caught sight of Nathan watching TV. Her voice had a sharp edge as she invited me into the kitchen. 'I don't believe he actually did it!'

I screwed my mouth tight, looking for a follow-on. What didn't she believe? That Arnie Mercury was the killer, or that he'd just taken his own life?

'He really went ahead and hanged himself!'

OK, got it. It struck me as a somewhat weird remark, in that it struck the same false note as Arnie himself when we'd talked on the train. I mean his comment earlier that morning, 'Why did she have to put up the five thousand? . . . Mary Beth didn't have to do that.' Then the garbage about God punishing the killer in his own way.

Mrs Fiorello seemed to be thinking out loud. 'It's a horrible thing to do . . . terrible. What it must take to plan something like that; the mechanics of it, finding the right equipment . . . just awful!'

Why the distress over her husband's killer? I didn't get it. Then I recalled that the two of them, Mary Beth and Arnie, were members of the same church. So I guessed they knew each other pretty well and shared the same beliefs, hence the concentration on his death.

But still, where was the relief that the case was suddenly solved, or the anger against Arnie? Shouldn't she feel doubly betrayed by a guy who was not only a friend but a fellow Christian?

Maybe it all ran too deep. Maybe if you're in shock, you don't think the way people expect. You go down little nooks and crannies of the brain. 'Arnie left a note,' I offered helpfully.

She gave me that sharp, inquisitive look. 'Did you read it?'

'That's why I came to see you. I thought you'd want to know. He said he was sorry.'

The look penetrated like a laser. 'Tell me exactly what the letter said. Was it a suicide note?'

'I guess.'

'Did he say he'd killed himself?'

I thought hard. 'He said he didn't have much longer to live, and that was a good thing.' Was that the same as saying he was gonna hang himself? 'There was a lot about God calling him and so forth,' I recalled.

She took a quick, deep breath. 'Sounds like suicide to me.'

'Me too.'

'What about the police?'

'Yeah, the cop I spoke with has it down as Arnie killing

himself,' I assured her. 'Isn't that the way they told it to you?'

Mrs Fiorello frowned and rubbed her temple like there was bad pressure building up; a migraine headache maybe. 'Death by hanging,' she muttered. 'They said they were looking at a connection between this and John's death. But go ahead, Joey, what else was in the note?'

I drew breath, went on as best I could. 'He apologised. To his family, to you and your family. And I think he meant it, Mrs Fiorello.' In a suicide note, what reason would you have to lie?

She closed her eyes and tilted her head back. 'Arnie's sorry!'

Arnie's dead. No more crazy voices.

My visit to the Fiorellos' house was intended to draw a line.

The next move was to find Kate and Connie to pass on the good news. Cancel the reward; Kurt was in the clear.

Once she was sure I'd told her everything in the note, Mrs Fiorello thanked me and showed me out. 'Joey, you've been really kind. I appreciate your coming. Not everyone would've taken the trouble.'

You hook the polite stuff on to the rough edges of the very worst situations to help you through. I said, 'That's OK. I wanted to help.' Smoothing and soothing, easing out through the hall.

She smiled through her trouble. Noble, gracious. Joan of Arc. 'Thank you.'

I glanced at the low telephone table beside a tall bookcase, noted a list of frequently used numbers sticky-taped to the front of the telephone directory. I looked twice at the list, written on rose-bordered, pink notepaper.

Identical. Roses – pink – a weird choice for a guy like Arnie to write his suicide note on, I thought at the time.

'Bye, Joey.' Mary Beth Fiorello showed me through the door with that sad, restrained smile.

I was out in the square, shell-shocked.

Boom!

You think it's finished, there's a moment of calm. Then the whole thing goes up in your face all over again!

9

'Log on, Kate!' Zoey waved her hands across my line of vision. 'Whoo-hoo, is anybody home?'

'What? Yeah, sorry.'

It was Monday. School was buzzing with talk of Arnie's suicide, rumour plus the odd hard fact, but I wasn't really into it. I had other things like Kurt still on my mind.

'I said, I'm glad the whole thing's over with,' Zoey repeated, mouthing what everyone else was saying. 'It means Mrs Fiorello can hold the funeral service Thursday with relative peace of mind, knowing the killer's not still roaming the streets.'

'Yeah, cool.'

'Y'know something; I always had Arnie Mercury down as a weirdo. The way he walked along, jerking his head. And he never used to say hi or anything.'

I sighed and shook my head. 'Leave it out, please.'

'What did I say?' Zoey bristled and appealed to Ziggy for support. 'I'm saying about Arnie. He was one strange guy!'

Zig agreed with Zoey, as always. 'Joey told me he got

five years for overdosing his old lady on morphine.'

'So axing the principal came easy to him.' Austin got in on the act with his own special brand of tactlessness. He took Zoey and Zig off down the corridor, going into detail all over again about the site superintendent's suspicious behaviour after he committed the crime. 'I was there!' he reminded them, with a touch of poetic licence. 'And boy, was his reaction strange!'

'. . . Kate?'

This time it was Carter's voice dragging me back from the Kurt conundrum. I'd just privately asked myself for the hundredth time how the cops would deal with the bloody footprint evidence now that Arnie had confessed and hanged himself. Bearing in mind the fact that Arnie Mercury never set foot on a rock face in his life.

Carter closed his locker door and came over to mine. 'I said, where were you when I needed you?'

'Don't, Joey. Not now.'

'Don't what?'

'Don't fool around. I'm not in the mood.' I turned to walk away.

Carter stayed by my locker. 'I wasn't fooling.'

I blinked hard, sighed and turned. For some reason I felt exhausted. 'You needed me . . . when?'

'Yesterday afternoon.' He stared at me across the

emptying locker room, his blue eyes deadly serious.

'Hey, listen; it wasn't me who didn't show up at Connie's house. We waited for you for over an hour!'

Still staring, coming up close, he told me privately, so that no one else could hear, that he had been the one who found Arnie in the store-room.

'Jeez, Joey, why didn't you call me? I was back home by eight. You could've called!'

'I had things to think about.'

'So? I would've come over, talked them through.' I was angry with him for not asking for help, so I tugged at his shirt sleeve, trying not to raise my voice. 'What things? Give me a for instance!'

'The suicide note. There's something bugging me.'

Two people whispering in a locker room attracts attention. Connie had seen us. Zoey and Zig had escaped from Austin and were retreading their steps. They ignored the bell for lessons and kept on heading our way.

'Tell me quick!' I hissed at Carter.

'First, the note doesn't actually state that he killed Fiorello,' he gabbled. 'Then there's the notepaper. He wrote the note on flowered paper . . .' Glancing up, he saw that Connie was in earshot, so he stopped.

'What?' She looked from Joey to me. 'So tell us the big secret!'

I sighed again, tried to be diplomatic for Connie's

sake. 'Carter has reasons to doubt what everyone's saying about Arnie.'

He frowned and ducked his head.

'Oh, come on!' Connie stood, hands on hips. 'Oh, Joey, don't give me that! Arnie killed Fiorello, then he took his own life. End of story!'

I knew she wanted it this way; nice and neat, with Kurt off the hook. We'd left him the night before, calmer than when he'd first explained about the two pairs of climbing shoes, but still pretty upset. I mean, it looked clear to us now that his own father had been the one to tread blood over Fiorello's carpet, for God's sake.

Which begged a couple of serious questions.

A second lesson bell jangled overhead. Kids darted across the locker room, ran down corridors into classrooms.

'Kate, tell Carter not to screw things up!' Connie pleaded. 'If the cops are happy to close the case now that Arnie confessed, why not let the whole thing drop?'

I was caught. Yeah, I could see her point. On the other hand, what Carter just told me cast doubt on Arnie's involvement (even if I didn't understand the thing about flowered notepaper) and chimed in with my own feeling about the unexplained footprint clue.

To put it bluntly: if I was the cop in charge of the investigation, I wouldn't be closing the file just yet.

'Kate!' Connie appealed a second time.

I backed away. 'What can I say?'

'Tell Joey to lay off! Tell him it's important . . . No, forget that; don't tell him anything! He'll only screw up!'

'Hey, Connie, cool it.' Zoey stepped up to take the heat out of the situation.

Connie was yelling at me and pointing at Carter. He looked to me for answers which I couldn't give. I'd sworn to Kurt that I wouldn't tell a soul that I'd seen him. Not even Joey. I didn't like to keep Carter in the dark because when I thought about it, we pretty well shared everything. But I'd given my promise.

'She's upset,' was all I could tell him.

I saw the look of disappointment. Not only had I not been there for him when he found poor Arnie (OK, so no one could blame me for that), but it was obvious to him that I was keeping something important from him now.

I tried to meet his gaze as Zoey and Zig ushered Connie down the corridor. They left us standing alone in a shaft of light between dark shadows from the rows of lockers.

Carter waited a few seconds for me to explain.

I clutched my books and shrugged my shoulders.

It was one of those times when looks screamed louder than words.

Complete silence.

Me pleading with him to accept that my lips were sealed. Joey's eyes telling me that I was letting him down big-time.

So, my day wasn't terrific.

While Zoey, Zig and especially Connie went along with the Arnie theory (site superintendent has secret history of paranoid schizophrenia, turns into homicidal maniac and cuts school principal into small pieces before taking his own life), I had doubts bubbling to the surface through English, social science, lunch break and maths.

Question one was to do with motive. I mean, I could think of three people with a better reason to kill Fiorello than Arnie. First, there was Don Silvermann, dropping in early to confront the principal over Kurt's exclusion, flying into a rage, committing the murder and squelching footprints all over the rug. I thought that forensics should definitely go back in there and measure the prints over again; vital clue, were they size eleven or size twelve?

Second, I couldn't get Dyanne Starr out of my head. Say she knew Fiorello was never gonna leave his wife. She would beg and plead and threaten. No way. Fiorello wanted to end the relationship, which would push Starr over the edge. She's the extreme type; if she couldn't get what she wanted, maybe she'd rather see Fiorello dead than let anyone else have him. Like, he was a possession, not a human being. I could see her thinking that way.

Third (and I hated myself for the way this one kept popping up), I kept on considering Mary Beth Fiorello.

A wife had been known to kill a husband for less than John Fiorello had done to her. He'd betrayed her and his kids. And Mary Beth was hot on honour, honesty, faithfulness, all those biblical, Ten Commandment things, including, 'Thou shalt not commit adultery'.

There again, 'Thou shalt not kill'.

So I doubted that she would bloody her own hands.

Besides, she was physically small and slight. So was Starr. Fiorello could probably have overcome either one of them, even given the fact that they'd grabbed Arnie's axe and were wielding it over his head.

This brought me back full circle to Don Silvermann, and the little I knew about him, beyond the public image.

('Kate, do you have a problem with this exercise?' Mrs Foreman asked me.)

Don Silvermann beat up his kids.

Don Silvermann just tried to get his wife certified as crazy.

('Kate? Are you feeling OK?' The maths teacher

leaned over my table, sliding my book away to discover that I hadn't answered a single question.)

Don Silvermann lied every opportunity he got.

The teacher put a hand on my shoulder. 'Why don't you take a little time out?' she said gently. 'We're all finding it difficult to cope with what's going on, so I understand what you must be going through.'

I looked up at her in a dumb, hazy way, I guess.

'Go home,' she insisted.

All the other kids were staring my way. Carter, who hadn't spoken to me all day, sat across the room, looking over his shoulder and frowning.

'I have to do the sound for *Death of a Salesman* tonight,' I reminded Mrs Foreman, struggling back into the here and now.

She nodded. 'All the more reason to go get some rest.' Closing my books, she guided me towards the door. 'I'll tell Miss Starr you'll be back in time for the performance, OK?'

So I was back home early afternoon, feeling light-headed and kind of disorientated. My dad was working and the house was quiet. Across the square, a cop car drove up and parked outside Mrs Fiorello's house. Krystal answered the door and two plain clothes detectives went in.

Boy, would I have liked to be a fly on that wall.

The phone rang. Maybe Joey checking in with me. I picked it up and said hi.

The caller clicked off without speaking. Two minutes later, the doorbell rang and I was still hoping that it was Carter going out of his way to say sorry for the way he'd been acting and wanting to know if I was gonna be OK in time for tonight. So I rushed to open the door.

Don Silvermann stepped inside before I had a chance to shut it again.

You know it's not a social visit when the guy pushes you against a wall and traps you there with his forearm across your throat.

I reached for the phone, knocked it from its cradle on to the hall floor. Silvermann trod on it hard and crushed it with the heel of his shoe. *The* shoe, actually. The sight of it was what made me more scared than the amount of force he was using to keep me pinned against the wall.

'Where's Kurt?'

'I don't know!'

More pressure against my neck. My head went right back, my hair caught in the light fitting on the wall.

'Sure you do. Where is he?'

I fought back. 'Lay off! I'll tell the cops!'

'And I'll deny it.' He towered over me, jerking my head sideways so that the hair tangled in the light pulled hard at my scalp. 'I've been watching you all day, Kate Brennan. I saw you leave the house and go into school. You left early. I followed you back here.'

'Let go of me! Why? What did I do?'

'You know where my son is!'

'No!'

'Say that once more and I'll break your neck!' He bounced me back against the wall, pummelling the air out of my lungs. 'You came snooping round my place looking for him. Afterwards, you found him and he told you stuff about me, didn't he?'

I stared back, saw from the look in his eyes that he didn't care how much he had to hurt me to get the information he wanted. 'Yeah,' I admitted. 'I heard how you were with your kids.'

'What did he do? Did he come across with the poor little beaten-up kids scenario? And you believed him?'

The guy's hairy, muscular arm was throttling me. 'Yeah, I believed him!'

Silvermann squeezed what felt like the last breath out of me. 'You take me to him, you hear!'

My bad day had turned to nightmare. I was slipping to the floor, losing consciousness, when I managed to nod my head.

Next thing I knew, I was in his car, directing him through the snarl-ups of mid-afternoon traffic, downtown to the tall concrete landmark of Fortune City Hospital.

10

Arnie Mercury writes a suicide note on Mary Beth Fiorello's stationery.

Jeez, that was weird.

No, wait. Arnie and Mary Beth had a mutual friend who gave them identical notepaper as a Thanksgiving gift.

How about that?

No. You wouldn't give a guy rose-bordered pink.

The paper belonged to Mary Beth for sure.

Mary Beth hadn't been to church yesterday morning; Krystal told me that. How did that slide into the picture? Dunno, but hang on to that slippery little fact. Figure it out.

Go through Sunday a.m.; action replay.

I lock up. I return the keys. Hanging man.

I visit Mrs Fiorello to offer whatever comfort a suicidal, screwy, homicidal maniac's (as I thought at the time) apology can bring. The widow quizzes me about the contents of the suicide note.

And now I think about it, it's like there's a funeral shroud over the whole Fiorello household. You can't breathe in there. The kids are programmed over what to say, and therefore what not to say. Mary Beth is hanging on to her self-control like a rock climber rappelling down a sheer cliff face. One slip and she smashes to her death.

('Joey, did you call Kate?')

What is she afraid of? Or rather, what does she have to hide? And why did she supply Arnie with the rose-bordered paper?

('Did you hear what I said, Joey? How's Kate?')

I walked the long corridor towards the locker room to make a phone call, pitching myself so many questions that I didn't register Connie running along beside me.

Finally, as I reached the phone booth, she stood right in front of me. 'I'm worried about Kate!' she gasped.

I nodded. 'Me too. I'm gonna call her.'

'Kate never gets sick!' Connie wailed. 'I guess it's my fault. She already had enough hassle over this Fiorello thing. I never should've taken her to see Kurt!'

I practically dropped the phone then, before I dialled. 'You did what?'

Connie screwed her eyes tight shut. 'Yeah. This was during the time you were finding your second body. I made Kate come with me to talk sense into Kurt,' she muttered. 'Only, by the time he'd filled us in on everything his wonderful father did, we were all three jibbering idiots. We came away total wrecks; Kate and me. And now we don't know what to do.'

OK, I didn't understand any of this. 'This is what Kate had sworn not to tell me?'

So now I felt lousy for giving her a hard time. I should've known there was a good reason Kate wasn't sharing everything she knew with me. I should've trusted her.

Connie lowered her voice to a husky whisper. 'Joey, I know it doesn't make sense, but Kate and I learned something important about the footprints in Fiorello's room. From what Kurt had to tell us, we think Don Silvermann is the killer!'

Jesus, I picked up the phone again fast! I punched in Kate's number. 'C'mon, answer!' I begged.

Nothing but the dialling tone. No answer machine message; nothing.

'OK, we pay her a visit,' I told Connie. 'We find out why she's not answering the phone.'

A normal Monday, late afternoon. Connie and I stood on the broad stoop outside Kate's big, white house, sheltering under the stone porch from the fat splashes of heavy rain whirling down from a windswept sky. I'd rung the bell three times. A guy trying to deliver a parcel addressed to Kate's dad had already given up and gone back to his car.

'She's not in!' Connie muttered, as screwed up as me by this time.

Where, other than home, would Kate go after she left school early with a sick note from Mrs Foreman? Possibly to see Sean at work in the studio. Maybe that was where we'd try next, only I wanted to take one look inside the house, just to be sure.

I went down a couple of steps into the rain, looked up at the front windows on the first storey for lights switched on or any other sign of life. I tried peering into the dark, street-level rooms. Everything quiet as the grave.

'Stand back, I'm gonna climb the railing and take a look through that small window over the door,' I told Connie. The window was semi-circular, with spokes of fancy ironwork shaped like a fan. Kate's house is nineteenth century, part of original Fortune City and a museum piece.

'What can you see?' Connie hissed up at me as I balanced on the spiked railing.

'Zilch.' An empty hallway, black and white chequered tiles . . . the phone smashed to pieces on the floor.

'Something happened!' I jumped down and told Connie to find the nearest public phone booth. I explained about the shattered phone. 'Call Kurt!' I yelled at her, dragging her across the square and into an empty booth. The rain splattered against the glass hood and raced down the nearby gutter. A cab splashed through a puddle by the kerb and soaked me as I stood and waited for Connie to make the call.

'What has this got to do with Kurt?' she demanded, gluing the phone to her ear with a trembling hand. She'd turned white, the dark make-up around her startled eyes making her look like an old-time silent movie star when the train is rushing along the track towards her.

'Don't ask me. Maybe nothing. It's the first thing that came into my head, that's all!' I was shivering from the wet and cold, and from the fact that I knew in my guts that Kate was in serious trouble.

'He's not answering,' Connie whimpered. My fear had crept under her skin. 'I'm getting a message telling me he's turned off his cell phone, but that can't be right. Kurt uses the phone charger in the office and keeps it switched on twenty-four hours a day, in case his mother tries to contact him.'

'OK, what's the fastest way you can take me to him?' I asked her.

She stared at me with her scared panda eyes. 'Downtown in a cab. Do you have any dough?'

I nodded, hailed the cab and hustled Connie in out of the rain.

'City Hospital,' she gasped.

Surmising from the way we were shaking and jabbering that we knew someone who'd just been rushed to the ER in a wailing ambulance, the guy put his foot down. He jumped a red light, took a couple of back streets, broke the limit down the freeway alongside the park.

'Stay cool, huh,' he told me sympathetically as he drew up at the hospital and took my money. 'You never know, man. Things might work out. If there's been an accident, they can sew stuff back on, put in new, plastic bits that you wouldn't believe!'

Following Connie down a basement corridor, I prayed to myself that the cab driver was more right than he knew. Things might work out. We could find Kate and Kurt deep in the kind of conversation that only Kate gets into; her convincing him that he should go to the cops and tell them all he knew, and that as long as he gave them the truth, he had nothing to worry about.

I'd be jealous then, because you just have to be in a room with Kate to know she's special, and I hate other guys falling in love with her, which they do often, only luckily so far Kate hasn't felt the same way about the guys – but then again it might only be a matter of time . . .

Connie passed a row of offices for well known charities. We heard the hum of photocopiers and fax machines, the tap of keyboards. People came and went along the corridor.

'This is it,' she told me, outside a door that had had its name plate removed. The door stood open four or five inches, so I pushed it further with my forefinger and stepped inside.

The place was wrecked. Grey fungus grew on the walls, water oozed from a burst pipe. And also, the equipment stacked on the table was scattered across the floor. There were upturned plastic chairs, wire trays, a disconnected phone. 'What happened here, World War Three?' I asked Connie.

She stood marooned in the chaos. 'We're too late!'

'Silvermann got here before us?' I stood a chair upright, rescued a smashed coffee machine from under the table. This was Mary Celeste stuff; you climb on board expecting to find out what happened to the crew, and all you get is a feeling that ghosts are crowding in on you from beyond this life, and you're failing to hear what they have to say.

Connie turned to me in total panic. 'Joey, what're we gonna do?'

'Ask somebody.' I turned, went out of the room, back down the corridor, poking my head into first this office, then that. 'Did anyone here see Kurt Silvermann?' I asked, up-front and laid-back as I could make it.

'– Nope.'

'– Who?'

'– Karen Silvermann's kid? No, sorry.'

No one was interested. It was strictly keep-your-head-down-and-don't-look-for-trouble time.

'Did you see what went off in the empty Childscape room?' I asked the woman in a cancer charity place. She was more helpful than the rest.

'No. I heard something, though. Were they moving furniture?'

'Yeah, kinda.'

She looked up from her desk and smiled. 'Right. I guessed that must be it. Though I didn't expect Don Silvermann himself to come and roll up his sleeves.'

'He was here?' Result! I beckoned Connie to join me quick. 'Who was he with?'

'I only recognised him from the pictures you see in the papers. He never came to Karen's office before.' The woman seemed to have plenty of spare time. I guess talking to me and Connie was better than franking envelopes. 'He's more into the art world and big business, they say. She's the one who gives her time.'

'Who was Mr Silvermann with?' I repeated.

The charity worker gave a small frown. 'Let me think. He arrived with a girl: tall, slim, long dark hair. He left half an hour later with the same girl and his son, Kurt.'

'Silvermann is totally evil!' Connie hammered home the reason why I should be worried. 'The only way he'd get Kurt and Kate to leave that bulding with him is by using force.'

Don't push it, Connie, I don't need you to tell me what I already know.

We'd left the hospital and were running along rain-drenched streets towards the Roosevelt Building. Fortune City is home to three million people, so looking for Kate, Kurt and his father could be needle-in-a-haystack stuff, unless you read into the situation and tried to second guess what you would have done in their situation.

'What's top of Silvermann's must-do list?' I'd asked Connie as we came away from the Childscape office.

'Finding his wife,' came the instant reply. 'He has to stop her and Elouise from breaking the news about how he tried to have Karen locked away in an asylum. But he can't do that until he finds out where she is. And Kurt is his only route to discovering that . . .'

'Yeah.' I'd got that. 'What would it take to get Kurt to tell his father what he needs to know?'

'He never would!' she'd insisted. 'Kurt's not scared of his father any more. He wouldn't ever betray his mom!'

'How about threatening someone else?' I'd suggested. 'If Silvermann put pressure on Kate, if he put her life on the line, would Kurt still hold back the information?'

That had been when Connie had turned pale again. She'd given no reply, and that had been when I'd come up with the Roosevelt Building.

Out of desperation, because it was the only other place I knew where Silvermann hung out.

Which is why, when we passed through the revolving glass doors into the marble and wood panelled lobby, and dripped rainwater all over the doorman's polished floor, I felt we were down to our very last chance of finding Kurt and Kate unharmed.

11

You can be terrified of a guy and still have a small corner of your mind operating, wondering why is he doing this? Or, I can. Maybe others would disagree, and say they spent their whole time paralysed with fear, their brain turned to jello.

In any case, I was trying to work Silvermann out as he took me downtown in his Mercedes and smarmed his way into a slot in the hospital car park normally reserved for surgeons visiting from out of town. He has a face, a figure, clothes, even a voice that jockeys in car lots automatically say 'yes sir, no sir' to. And they recognise the Silvermann name.

So he was parked and marching me towards Kurt's hiding-place with minumum trouble, his arm slotted through mine like I was his favourite niece.

He didn't need to warn me not to make a run for it; the pressure was there in his grasp, and the look of steel behind the easy smile.

I did try to attract attention as we entered the dim lobby leading to the corridor lined with charity headquarters. But who reads terror on a girl's face when a guy like Don Silvermann greets them? Hi there, how're you doing? What did you guys do to the weather to make it pour with rain all day?

And so on. I was dragging my heels as we approached the flood-damaged room, even twisting a little in his grasp. But we were too near now to throw him off the track. I slumped and let him shove me through the door.

Click; it closed behind me. Kurt came out from the inner room, ready to repel intruders. Then shock deactivated him.

Father stared at son. I saw the resemblance between them; Don thirty years on from Kurt's flawless face, but still the athlete, still handsome.

Kurt shot me a look of pure hatred, which Don picked up.

'There you go, hothead. Jumping to conclusions.' Silvermann manufactured a smile. 'Kate isn't here voluntarily. I had to – er – persuade her.'

Strange that he needed to put that right. Unexpected too that he should withhold the threats and turn to wheedling.

'Son!' he said, going closer to where Kurt stood still in shock. 'I need to find your mother to talk with her. She and I haven't communicated well lately, that's all. Now, you can help by telling me where she is.'

Don't fall for that old line!

'Kurt, I don't know what Elouise told you about Dr Grainger, but give me a chance to explain. The guy's big in his field of psychiatry; he's one hundred per cent convinced that your mom will benefit from long-term hospitalisation.'

Yeah, don't listen! I transmitted my thoughts hard as I could to Kurt, who stared stoney-faced at his grovelling father.

'You see, it's for her own sake. She can't control her drinking, and it's damaged her view of reality. She suffers these paranoid delusions about me, which Elouise has taken on board. But you won't, will you, Kurt? You know I wouldn't do anything to harm your mother.'

The guy believes his own garbage! This idea was new to me and it struck me hard. *To him, his lies aren't lies; they're the absolute truth!*

'Screw you!' Kurt muttered, mustering his own vivid memories of the damage Don Silvermann was capable of.

Silvermann's voice took on a harder edge. 'Look at it another way. If any of this stuff gets out and the press grabs hold of it, think what it would do to our family name.'

Kurt laughed and turned away. 'Yeah, I really care about *that*!'

'Well, maybe you don't, but your mom does.'

I rated this as much smarter of Silvermann; playing on Kurt's weak point, which was his love for his mom.

'Do you want her to be dragged down and humiliated by what they write about us? They'll focus in on her alcoholism, believe me; "Queen of Kids' Charity Turns to Booze!" So don't you think it would be better if you let me know where she is so we can begin to talk things through in private like sensible adults?'

For a moment Kurt hesitated. It was true, he would want to protect Karen. So he glanced at me with a question in his eyes.

I shook my head. 'No way!' I breathed.

Silvermann–Jekyll snapped into Silvermann–Hyde. He turned on me, swiping at my head with the flat of his hand. I ducked as he lunged, plunging against the table and sending stacks of stuff crashing to the floor. 'You keep your nasty little face out of this!' he snarled, cornering me and shoving Kurt backwards as he leaped in to defend me.

Furniture scraped along the floor as Kurt staggered; I launched myself out of the corner, kicking up at Silvermann's groin, trying out the karate self-defence moves you read about in women's manuals. Two against one; Kurt and I stood a good chance.

Until his father pulled the gun.

He'd been doubled over with pain, giving Kurt and me time to stumble over the scattered chairs and files to regroup by the door. We were just about out of there!

But not quite. Silvermann managed to stand upright clutching the gun he took out of a holster fitting snugly under his arm. He aimed it right at me. 'You're dead!' he promised.

We froze. 'Froze' is an overused word in this context, but it's accurate, believe me. I didn't move a muscle with that silver barrel pointing at my head.

Back in control, Kurt's father gave a smug grin. I would say that was *his* weak point, his Achilles heel: smugness. In fact, the guy was so arrogant it oozed out of his pores. It coloured every sentence and blinded him to the fact that what he said now could be taken down and later used in evidence against him.

Did you ever know anyone so crazily big-headed? Me neither. But think of those politicians from the president downwards who do stupid things ('I did *not* have sexual relations with that woman!'), either because they grew so powerful that they think they're above the law, or because they have a posse of little men in big suits scurrying around after them to clean up the mess.

Don Silvermann was in that category, so he didn't care what he told us in Karen's office that might incriminate him later.

Anyway, who knows, maybe he had it in his mind to kill us.

'You wouldn't believe what my family has put me

through during this last week,' he began, gun directed steadily at my head. 'First, there's this problem with Karen. If the woman had put herself into the hands of the best doctors and let them treat her personality disorder the way I wanted them to, you, my dear, wouldn't be in this mess now.'

I tried not to shake and cave in under pressure. Only, it was scary because he was so calm, and the gun didn't move a fraction of an inch.

'The problem is, Elouise and Kurt have always taken their mother's side, right from the start. They don't see that I try to do my best for them. Take this problem with Fiorello, for instance. I get back to the apartment on Wednesday, looking for Kurt so I can wrestle out of him information about where his mother and sister have decided to run off to, and what do I find? The kid only got himself excluded from school!'

I was scarcely breathing by this time. I concentrated on the guy's mouth spouting explanations. Full mouth pursing and puckering, then pulled out at the corners in a fake smile, then moving again, taking us back five days to a homicide in a room in a school . . .

'Some might say, "Tough! Let the kid stew in his own juice. I got more important things to do!" But not me. I'm angry with the guy who decided to do this to my boy. I find time to call him, leave a message setting up a meeting. Then I put down the phone and I'm still upset. I'm not even supposed to be in Fortune City, for Christ's sake.' Silvermann's gaze flicked sideways to Kurt. 'The story is that I'm in Boulder, Colorado with your mom, right?'

Kurt nodded warily. He was looking for a chance to jump his father, but Silvermann noticed the coiled spring position.

'You too, Kurt. You're dead if you make a move!'

He was genuine, I swear.

'You wanna hear what I decided to do next?' he asked me. 'Direct action is what I believe in, isn't it, Kurt? I admit, I gave the kid a hard time for bringing the family name down in the eyes of the school. Plus, I was angry with him for refusing to divulge information about his mom. So we had an argument.

'After the argument, I was still upset with Mr Fiorello. Angry enough to get in the car and drive right over, tell the guy I think he was premature excluding my son. Explain how Kurt was training for Pikes Peak in the New Year, not even expecting that maybe it's too late in the day to find a school principal behind his desk.'

Silvermann stopped to laugh at a private joke.

I held my breath. We were coming to the axe bit, and the Jackson Pollock drips and dribblings of blood on the walls.

'In fact, Fiorello wasn't *at* his desk. He was *under* it!'

Kurt jerked his head back, grabbed at me. I swayed slightly, kept myself upright. Silvermann wasn't through yet; not by a long way.

'Quite a mess,' he admitted. 'Not what I was expecting when I pushed my way in there. A body, a weapon, a catatonic guy crouched in the corner.'

Who? Who, for God's sake! Silvermann had slowed right down to savour the horror on our faces. My head was throbbing, my mouth was dry.

'It made my day! Not only do I stumble across a homicide, but the killer. And I'm not even officially in town. My first thought, I admit, is, "What will the media do with this? They'll find a way to smear me and involve me in a crime I didn't even commit!" Mud sticks to people in my position, but there are ways of ducking and dodging around it. My second thought is, "I've gotta put a lid on this!" So I proceeded to cut a deal with the guy with the axe.'

'Who was it?' I ignored the breathtaking selfishness of all this and risked opening my mouth because if I didn't, my head would burst.

'What was the guy's name? The school janitor — Mercury. Arnie Mercury.'

Arnie! My heart took a dive, plummeted through the soles of my feet. *After all this; Arnie!* We kept on coming back to the same name. I wanted to cry and crumple on the floor. I would have done except that

Silvermann had a gun aimed at my head.

'I discovered he couldn't move from the corner. He'd done the deed and was completely out of it. And he kept babbling about the voices in his head, how they'd told him to "deliver her from evil". It made no sense to me at first, but the only way to get him to move was to keep him talking. I'm guiding him across the room, over the corpse and the murder weapon, saying "Who's 'her'?" "Mary Beth," he replies. He tells me he's saving Mary Beth from her evil husband because God told him to.

'It was pretty clear to me the guy's crazy, and no way were we talking divine intervention. Voices – schmoices. It turns out, as I talk to this pathetic guy, that Fiorello had been fooling around with another woman and the wife was angry. She's some kind of religious nut, like Mercury, so she manages to persuade him that he's hearing the voice of God telling him to kill her husband.'

'Mary Beth persuaded him? How do you know that?' I gasped.

Silvermann, cool throughout, now showed minor irritation. 'Look, it's not important. I had to talk him through it and let him think he'd just acted as the hand of God, so I heard a whole heap of garbage about this Mary Beth; how she told Arnie that God was displeased with Fiorello for having numerous affairs. She made him truly believe that her husband deserved to die because of his adultery. (God, we'd all be dead men if that was true!) What's more, she personally nominated Arnie to do God's work by convincing him that Christ himself had appeared to her in a vision and named the poor guy as his instrument of justice.'

I shook my head and let myself slump back against the door as the truth sank in. I saw Arnie as an automaton waiting for someone to come along and press his buttons.

And Mary Beth as the controller. Control freak. Putting voices in Arnie's head.

'I never met a guy so easy to manipulate,' Silvermann admitted. 'When I told him God would be pleased with him, and that he mustn't tell a single soul what he'd done here, or mention the fact that I'd shown up to help him, he agreed with every word I said.

'I told him it had to be our secret, and Mary Beth's, and that he must change out of the clothes he was wearing and burn every item in the school's incinerator. A little later, he must come back as if nothing had happened. Do his job, go about his business, and never say a word. He went off like a lamb to do as I said. Yeah, a lamb!'

From and to the slaughter.

Killer as victim.

That was a new one on me.

'You disgust me!' Kurt told his father.

He knew it would flip him into monster mood again, but he was past caring.

There was more unplanned table-shifting. Don Silvermann beat Kurt with the butt of his gun, while I grappled with what was going on inside my head.

The gun won.

Silvermann ordered us out of the Childscape office, back to his car. He drove us to the Roosevelt Building, confident that we wouldn't hold out on him for much longer. Sooner rather than later, Kurt would be forced to divulge to him the whereabouts of Karen and Elouise.

12

Acne-man, alias the doorman at the Roosevelt Building, held Connie at bay with one pile-driver hand and punched me in the face with the other. He recalled from my earlier visits that he didn't like me.

I slammed back against the rosewood and walnut inlay, skidded forward across the grey marble, cannoned back into the guy and took a feeble swing.

'Joey!' Connie protested in a long-suffering, whining voice. 'There's no need to fight. Just tell him why we're here!'

Like, yeah! This security man had gold braid and gilt buttons for brains. He'd taken one look and decided we were undesirables. I would need a week to explain why it was essential for us to find Kurt and Kate. And then Parrot-man would come back with, 'Sorry. No visitors to the apartment. Mr Silvermann's orders!'

He was squaring up for another punch, so I had to invent an effective lie, and fast.

'We've got a message for Mr Silvermann about his wife,' Connie cut in. Her drama training really paid off. She was so convincingly practical and homey, Mrs Willie

Loman, that for a second she even had me fooled. And it worked great on the doorman too.

He lowered his massive fist and stood back. 'Why didn't you say? Hey, she didn't have an accident, did she?'

Connie nodded confidentially. 'Just a small one, in her car, nothing serious. We need to speak to her husband, please.'

Lump-head, dough-brain; why would two rain-drenched kids be trusted with this kind of message? But Connie deserved an Oscar, I'll give her that.

Anyway, he gave me the hard stare and told me to stay put. But he nodded at Connie to go ahead. 'Mr Silvermann just got back with Kurt and his girlfriend,' he confided to her as she waited for the elevator.

'Girlfriend'? Connie's calm mask slipped. She gave me a wobbly look.

'Forget it,' I whispered. As the door slid open, I shoved Acne-Man as hard as I could against the far wall, then stepped inside. Connie and I went up with a hydraulic hiss, leaving dough-features to labour up the stairs. 'Believe me, the last thing on Kurt's mind right now is regarding Kate as dateable material!'

I hoped. I reasoned: he's facing the fact that his father would let his only son stand accused of murder rather than tell the truth. That's a big issue to take along to your therapist some day.

Reassured, Connie looked on the bright side. 'At least we know they're here!'

Ping! The elevator reached the ninth floor.

'And still OK,' she added. 'Which is good, isn't it? . . . Joey, it's good that we tracked them down this far!'

I was too busy thinking to reply. There was the dove-grey door to the Silvermann apartment with its fisheye peephole allowing occupants to see who'd come visiting.

Fact number one: right now Don Silvermann wouldn't welcome guests.

Fact number two: this was the only official entrance, but the apartment was a duplex, with internal stairs to tenth floor level.

Fact three: we had to act fast.

'Ring the bell and draw their attention,' I told Connie. 'When Silvermann comes to the door, he won't let you in for obvious reasons, but try to keep him talking.'

She partly lost it then. 'What do I say?'

'You'll think of something.' I left her trembling and pushing the bell button, while I took the public stairs to the next floor.

I was relying on the Roosevelt Building providing access to an external fire escape from the central well that ran from basement to top storey. If I stepped out on to the metal stairway on the ninth, I could go up to the tenth and work out how it linked to the Silvermann's apartment at that level.

But this had to happen fast, while Connie distracted Silvermann. So I was up one flight of stairs, out on to the fire escape without noticing the rain. I worked my way along, stopping as I came to a window, peering inside the building, darting past and on to the next until I came to the one I calculated to be Kurt's place. One quick look inside at a bedroom; a pair of skis propped against the closet, sports clothing strewn across the floor, important art on the walls. Yeah, this looked like Kurt's place.

And *ker-ching*; the window was open half an inch! I edged my hands under the frame, fumbled, began to raise it. Then I bent low, straddled the sill, eased myself out of the wet into the dry, silently entered the Silvermann's apartment.

Waah-waah! Waah-waah!

An intruder alarm wailed into the silence.

I froze as footsteps rushed up the duplex stairs.

13

Silvermann moved Kurt and me from the Childscape office to the Roosevelt Building and went through the same Jekyll and Hyde tactics as before. Maybe more self-pitying when he pleaded, rougher when he threatened, and his temper was on an even shorter fuse.

And the gun was always there; across his lap when he sat at the desk underneath the O'Keefe painting and calmly told Kurt that he, Don Silvermann, would win in the end. He and Dr Erskine Grainger would convince the medical world that Karen was crazy, and as soon as he got his hands on his wife's wealth, he would make sure to cut Kurt off without a cent.

'Unless you start seeing things my way and tell me where she is!' he conceded.

Then the doorbell rang and he got up to use the fisheye to find out who it was. 'Someone to see you, Kurt.' Laid back as he returned to the chair, gun levelled at me, apparently regarding the interruption as a small amusement. 'Says her name's Connie. Little girl. Nice looking, but talks too much and not in your league, if you want my opinion.'

I saw Kurt make a move towards the door, then freeze on the spot when Silvermann swung the gun round and fixed it on him.

'I told her you weren't home.'

'Screw you!' Kurt yelled. Never mind the gun, he set off again for the door.

'Yeah, sure, invite her in!' Silvermann trained his aim on the door. 'The more the merrier!'

Kurt swore and hit out at the nearest thing: a giant blue and white Chinese vase in a recess by the door. It toppled and smashed into a thousand pieces.

Then, *waah-waah*! The intruder alarm came in on top of the crunching porcelain. Silvermann shot out of his chair, lunged at me and dragged me up the stairs.

We reached Kurt's room, me ahead of Silvermann, the gun pressed hard into the small of my back.

'Go ahead!' He shoved me forward into what looked like an empty, untidy room with its window wide open and the rain pouring in. 'Look behind the door!' Silvermann ordered, half-in, half-out of the doorway.

I did as he said. 'No one!'

The cream drapes blew in the wind, billowing into the room. Raindrops fell on to the bed, darkening the beige pillows. Silvermann yelled above the alarm for me to cross the floor and check out of the window. 'If anyone gets it, it's you!'

So I picked my way across Kurt's stuff until I felt the chill of the wind and the cold splashes of rain. I leaned out of the window, looked to left and right. 'Nothing!'

He made me climb out over the sill on to the metal landing, looking down over the rail, ten storeys to the yard below. Then he leaned out himself, and that was when Joey hit him.

He was clinging to the landing above our heads, hanging by both hands and ready to drop. As Silvermann climbed out, Joey landed his full weight on the guy's head and shoulders.

'He's got a gun!' I gasped, pressed back against the rail as they struggled.

It was a small space and a deadly drop, the rail at waist height. Any one of us could be forced over, any moment; just one slip on the wet surface would be enough.

Silvermann fired wild shots as Joey fought for the gun. Riding piggy-back, he leaned forward to grab the man's wrist. Like clumsy acrobats, with bullets bouncing off metal and brick, they toppled against the building and Joey slipped to the floor of the landing.

He was forcing the gun out of Silvermann's grip when I steadied myself against the rail and lashed out with my feet. The same trick as before. I landed a kick against his shin, the most vicious I could. I kicked again as his legs buckled, and again as he went down, sliding across the landing towards the edge, staring a ten storey drop in the face.

Joey had the gun. He pointed it at Silvermann's writhing body.

'Don't, Carter! Don't shoot!' I cried.

The intruder alarm filled our heads and brought cop cars screaming. Behind us, Kurt appeared with Connie in the frame of his bedroom window.

'What do you want me to do?' Joey yelled at Kurt, gun aimed at Don Silvermann's head as he lay belly-down on the fire escape landing. Rain lashed us. I shivered and shook uncontrollably, waiting for Kurt's reply.

'Give me the gun,' he said quietly. 'And get the hell out of here, Joey.'

Which wasn't what we were expecting. Carter frowned through the rain at me, then reluctantly handed over Silvermann's gun.

Kurt's father groaned and rolled on to his back. The sirens blared closer.

'I mean it, Joey; go! It's easier if you're not around when the cops get here.'

'So what?' Carter tried to figure it out. 'He gets away with taking you and Kate prisoner and holding you at gunpoint?'

Kurt shook his head. His hand was steady. 'He gets away with nothing, believe me. But you gotta let me handle it.'

At last, Joey agreed. He pulled me in through the window, ready to make a quick exit. 'Don't be crazy, OK?' he warned Kurt.

'No way, man.' Kurt knew what he planned to do to the guy still lying in the rain. Maybe he'd known all his life the kind of punishment he would hand out to his lousy father the first chance he got.

14

'Carter, where are we going? What about the first night; *Death of a Salesman*, remember?' Kate worried about letting people down, even at a time like this.

Starr was minus one leading lady, her sound technician and her lighting operator. It was six o'clock; an hour and a half before curtain-up.

'How could I forget?' I answered. 'But this won't take long!' Kate was the one who'd helped me make up my mind by telling me what Silvermann had revealed to her and Kurt about the voices in Arnie's head, and more specifically about the origin of those voices. Deliver her from evil by leading him into temptation. 'Her' equals Mary Beth Fiorello. 'Him' equals Arnie, poor sucker.

There was still time to do what I needed to do, then make it back to school. After that, we had a show to run, provided Connie recovered from seeing Kurt aiming a gun at Don Silvermann's head.

We'd left them in the apartment to deal with the cops. For a couple of seconds, I'd pictured Kurt blasting a hole in his father's skull. Crazy, but who could've blamed him?

Then I thought: no, Kurt has something smarter in mind, which his father will still be around to appreciate. Or not. Kurt's problem and Kurt's solution.

Meanwhile, I had the problem of Mary Beth Fiorello and a piece of rose-bordered pink notepaper.

'Is your mom home?' I asked Krystal.

The kid recognised me and slowly nodded from behind the chained door. 'I can't talk to you, and neither can Mommy.'

'Tell her I want to speak with her about Arnie Mercury.' Now that it came to it, there was no point dodging the issue. 'Tell her it's important.'

'Please!' Kate added.

Krystal frowned at her. She was only eight years old, but she was carrying a lot of tough stuff. 'Wait here,' she told us.

She came back after a while. 'Mommy's crying,' she told us.

'Let us in,' Kate coaxed. 'We only want to talk.'

So Krystal released the chain and we went inside. We found Mary Beth Fiorello curled up in a leather chair in what must have been her husband's study. The little girl showed us to the room, then slid away to child-mind Nathan next door.

What made Mary Beth finally cry?

If I could answer that I'd be the greatest psychologist

of the twenty-first century. I only know from her red and swollen eyes that she'd been like this for some time.

Kate's gentle side came out as she sat on the rug beside Mary Beth's chair and indirectly accused her of plotting her own husband's death.

A *gentle* accusation? So? Life is never simple.

Sure, Mary Beth was not what she seemed. She could, as Dyanne Starr had said, twist people around her little finger. And some would call her wicked.

True, Fiorello would still be alive if she hadn't brainwashed Arnie. But she also suffered.

Ask yourself later: *who do I really blame*?

'What will you do?' Mrs Fiorello asked Kate. She wasn't crying now. 'Will you inform the police?'

Silent, Kate looked up at me.

What was the crime exactly? Inciting a homicide. Is there such a thing? I guess so.

Mary Beth took a deep breath. 'Anything I tell you will sound as if I'm shirking my responsibility, but I do want you both to understand.'

Was she genuine? Don't ask me. I'd been there, discovering bodies, so you'd think I'd be wised up. Yet I'd been wrong one hundred per cent of the time.

'Can you imagine the pain?' she asked us. 'John's misbehaviour had been going on for years. There were fights, promises which he broke, more women . . . And he heaped on the humiliation. You remember last Thursday night?'

Kate nodded. 'Yeah, the rehearsal.'

When Fiorello had disappeared off the scene with Starr.

'To shame me and the children so publicly; in front of his students!' Mary Beth sighed, then fell to pieces again. 'It felt like the final straw. And that was when Arnie found me sobbing in John's empty office. He heard me say, God forgive me, that I wished my husband was dead!'

'Please!' Kate whispered. 'Don't cry any more.'

Mary Beth nodded and drew herself up. 'That was like a seed being planted. I felt the idea swell and grow. God too would wish to see John punished. He had offered him many, many chances to repent, and always John turned away from the Lord. And Arnie said he wanted to help me.' She turned her face up to me. 'You see, Joey, God speaks in mysterious ways!'

I found it easy to fend off this appeal to my spiritual side. 'So, if you set it up between you, and you stood back and let Arnie do it for you, why offer the reward?' I asked.

The grieving widow frowned. 'That's what people expect you to do.'

Well, that was straight down the line. The reward was a cover-up. Right.

'I did try to protect Arnie,' she pointed out. 'I made it clear that I didn't think he was the one. I told him, all we

134

needed to do was to stay calm and let the police follow other clues.'

'Didn't you worry about the footprints?' This interested me. 'Arnie must've told you that an outsider had stumbled on to the scene.'

Again she frowned, then nodded. 'He had no idea who it was, only that the guy had his reasons for keeping quiet. But anyhow, that was good, you see. It threw people off the track.'

Yeah, I conceded. It had pointed the finger straight at Kurt. I was still hung up on the pink paper. 'Did you also persuade Arnie to take his own life?'

'He was in despair,' she answered, her voice drained of emotion. 'I think he'd blocked out most of what he'd done, but his voices plagued him with doubts. I had to keep a close eye on him to make sure he didn't suddenly deviate from the plan we'd agreed.'

'You were scared he'd go to the cops?' Forgive the fact that I wasn't as gentle as Kate.

Mary Beth winced and turned her head away.

'So he was confused and scared,' I prompted. 'So how soon did it occur to you that the best thing was for him to take his own life?'

'I didn't suggest it,' she protested. 'That was his idea. My task was to convince him that everything had gone well so far. But when I saw him outside church yesterday I knew he'd reached rock bottom. So I took him away in the car, over to school to find a quiet place to talk.

'Only, he broke down and said a lot of things – Krystal and Nathan were there. I had to get him out fast and leave them in the car. Arnie and I went to his office. He said a hundred times he wished he was dead.'

She sighed again, hung her head, tore a paper tissue into shreds. 'I had to reconsider. I told him, perhaps that was right. Maybe God wanted to take him, maybe He was telling him it was time. But if he did put an end to his own life, he must be sure to leave a note making clear what he was doing and why, so that no one else would get the blame.'

'The notepaper?' I pressed her harder as her voice began to trail away to nothing. I needed this last piece of the puzzle more than you might expect.

She looked up at me more sharply. 'What about it?'

'You gave him the paper?'

A nod, a frown, more shredded Kleenex.

'Did you dictate word for word what he wrote?' I couldn't withold the scorn from my voice. Cry now, lady! Personally, I think it calls for plenty more tears.

'No! I found the pad in my purse. I handed a sheet to him, saying that I was certain he had God's blessing.'

'And left him in his office and drove home.' I turned and went out of the room, heard the TV, saw Krystal and Nathan watching me leave with big, scared eyes.

136

REQUIEM

(With apologies to Arthur Miller.)

The show went on.

Connie was excellent. She kissed Austin Wainwright without flinching and told those no-hopers, Biff and Happy, that the man deserved their respect.

The sound technician and the lighting operator did their best, given the difficult circumstances. (i.e. I missed one cue for Ben music and Carter missed a spotlight on Austin at the end of Act One.)

About Mary Beth?

Carter and I agreed we couldn't expose her. It was too harsh, and anyway who would take care of Krystal and Nathan if their mom was put in gaol?

I also agreed in theory with Carter that we shouldn't tear ourselves to pieces analysing it.

Let's say, the whole thing brought him and me closer than we'd been before, then made us drift further apart.

He'd been the one to put the veto on talking it through, whereas I sometimes felt I needed to.

Meanwhile, Mary Beth held up well at her husband's funeral against unsubstantiated rumours circulated by Dyanne Starr.

The gossip was that Arnie had been in thrall to Mary Beth and killed Fiorello under her command. 'In thrall'? It's a Starr expression. I met several people who believed her, and many others who chose not to.

I said nothing. Neither did Carter.

Eventually Mary Beth and the kids will move on to a new town, start over. Everyone will be relieved.

I think Kurt solved his problem better than Joey and I handled ours.

He cut a deal with his dad, hid the gun and told the cops that he activated the intruder alarm by mistake. Don Silvermann, fooled by the alarm, had fired random shots to warn off supposed felons. The cops went away complaining about idiot kids who climb out on to the fire escape without decommissioning the sensor.

The deal was this: Don Silvermann would quit hounding his wife. He would allow her to divorce him on her own terms. In return, Kurt would say nothing about the beatings, nothing about Erskine Grainger and the crooked diagnosis, or about his father's un-disclosed visit to Fiorello's office.

If Daddy refused, Kurt promised to bring Connie, me and Carter in as witnesses in a big court case where Don Silvermann would stand accused of abuse going back fifteen years. Even if he had the connections to get a 'not guilty' (which he probably did), the publicity would crucify him.

Rough justice. And it almost worked. Until a pernickety detective in the Fortune City Police Department decided he still wasn't happy about the bloody footprints on Fiorello's rug. He got Forensics to re-measure them on the scaled-down photographs, and came up with the information that they were size twelve, one size too big for Kurt. Which took the cop back to re-examine the store card evidence, and the discovery that, later in the same day, Don Silvermann had also bought an identical pair.

And this brought the police back to the Roosevelt Building. So, in the end the Silvermann name hit the headlines after all. For failing to disclose a homicide.

Carter doubts that the Silvermanns will ever recover their former status as Fortune's number one family. I say wealth like that absorbs scandal like a boxer takes a punch to the body. No problem. Don Silvermann will hire a good attorney. Newly-divorced, he'll be back and looking for rich wife number two.

'Cynic!' Carter tells me.

I laugh. He's the one with the jaundiced view of life, I say.

'I'm not, actually,' he protests, staring me straight in the eye. 'Far from it.'

I joke to sidestep the emotion I read behind his look. 'There we go, Carter; you and me fighting again!'